RAZOR WIRE

LAUREN GALLAGHER

RIPTIDE
PUBLISHING

Riptide Publishing
PO Box 6652
Hillsborough, NJ 08844
www.riptidepublishing.com

Razor Wire
Copyright © 2014 by Lauren Gallagher

Cover Art by L.C. Chase, lcchase.com/design.htm
Editor: Carole-ann Galloway
Layout: L.C. Chase, lcchase.com/design.htm

ISBN: 978-1-62649-188-5

First edition
December, 2014

Also available in ebook:
ISBN: 978-1-62649-187-8

RAZOR WIRE

LAUREN GALLAGHER

RIPTIDE
PUBLISHING

To the girls in blue.

TABLE OF CONTENTS

CHAPTER 1
KIM

T he door flew open, letting a gust of Okinawa's tropical wind into the air-conditioned front office of Naval Station White Beach's security precinct.

"MA3 Lockhoff."

The voice made my skin crawl. Gritting my teeth against a sudden wave of nausea, I looked up from the logbook I'd been updating. "Yes, Sir?"

The door banged shut behind Lieutenant Stanton as he took off his black-brimmed white cover. "My office. Now."

My heart dropped straight into my boots. It didn't help that the other three master-at-arms in the room had abruptly stopped talking. I thought I'd even heard their heads snap toward me.

This doesn't concern any of you, I wanted to snarl at them. Instead, I swallowed hard and managed to croak, "Yes, Sir. I'll be right there."

Without a word, he walked past the communal desk where I was sitting. I eyeballed the trash can beside me, wondering if I should just give in to the nausea now or wait until I was in his office. Even the thought of heaving my lunch onto his spit-shined black shoes couldn't relieve the tension in my gut, though.

"What the fuck was that about?" MA1 Gutiérrez barked from behind me.

I closed the logbook and then stood, but I couldn't make eye contact with him, so I busied myself adjusting my bulky police belt, which sat uncomfortably on my hips and lower back. "I don't know."

Liar, liar . . .

"You don't know?"

I couldn't continue to avoid eye contact unless I wanted to get reamed for insubordination, so I lifted my gaze. I hated the meek sound of my voice as I replied, "No, MA1."

Still hanging back against the wall, MA3s Keller and Barkley exchanged hushed words. Then they slipped out into the hallway connecting the shared office with the rest of the precinct.

Gutiérrez didn't even seem to notice they'd gone—he was busy staring me down. "What the fuck is going on, MA3?"

I swallowed again. He wasn't the type of lead petty officer who tolerated his people bypassing the chain of command. It was partly because it had a tendency to come back and bite him in the ass and partly because, well, what LPO wasn't on a bit of a power trip? And in this case, as far as he knew, I was leapfrogging him, Chief, *and* Senior Chief and going straight to the security officer. I might as well have pissed in his coffee in front of the entire command.

"I don't know, MA1." I spoke through clenched teeth to keep from throwing up. Or letting them chatter. "He didn't say."

You were right there. You heard him.

Please don't make me explain this.

Please, MA1 . . .

Gutiérrez's eyes narrowed. "So the SECO is just randomly calling you in for a one-on-one?" He waved a hand toward Stanton's office. "To chat about the weather?" The sarcastic undertone and the slightest lift of his eyebrow made my blood turn cold.

Did he know? If he did, then who else . . .

It took every bit of willpower I had not to glance to my left and make sure that trash can was still within reach. There was no point in breaking eye contact and giving myself away.

Right then, the phone on the desk rang. I almost jumped out of my skin. Gutiérrez rolled his eyes and gestured past me. "Answer that."

Not that I liked being treated like a secretary—that had gotten old a week into being one of only three women in the precinct—but at least it gave me an excuse to turn away.

And that trash can was still where I'd left it. Noted.

"CFAO White Beach, MA3 Lockhoff speaking. How may I—"

"My *office*, MA3." Stanton's voice was a low growl. "*Now.*"

"Yes, Sir."

The line went dead.

I hung up the receiver and took a deep breath, telling myself my mouth wasn't really watering. I wasn't really going to get sick and—

Behind me, Gutiérrez sighed impatiently.

And I couldn't stop it.

I dropped to one knee, grabbed the trash can with both hands, and vomited onto the crumpled papers and sandwich wrappers.

"Fuck!" Gutiérrez flew back a step as I threw up again. "What the hell?"

When I was sure nothing else would come up, I coughed and spat into the trash. "I'm sorry," I croaked. My head was still spinning, and now my face was burning, too.

One of Gutiérrez's boots appeared in my peripheral vision. Then the other. I closed my eyes, bracing for him to fly off the handle.

What I didn't expect was a hand on my shoulder.

"Hey. Lockhoff."

I cleared my burning throat and lifted my head, blinking my eyes into focus.

His expression had changed completely. All the sternness was gone; his eyes were wide and his forehead creased. I couldn't remember seeing so much concern on his face before, especially not seconds after he'd been ready to read someone the riot act.

In a gentle voice, he asked, "You okay?"

I nodded and sat back on my heels. "Yeah. I should . . ." I gestured at the trash can. "Shit. I need—"

"Lockhoff." When I looked up again, his eyebrows had pulled together. "Does this have something to do with why Stanton wants to see you?"

I let my face fall into my hands, and just as I couldn't hold back the nausea a moment ago, there was no stopping the tears. Shame. Fear. Nerves. God, I couldn't even put my finger on what it was. Could've been the fucking hormones for all I knew, but damn it, I wasn't ready to surrender anything to them yet.

"Hey. Easy." His voice was lower now, as if he'd knelt beside me. Then his arm was around my shoulders. "Take it easy."

I got my shit together as quickly as I could and wiped my eyes. "I didn't think anyone knew."

Gutiérrez sighed. "Rumors are what they are. They're—"

The phone on the desk rang again, startling me so bad I would've fallen if he hadn't held me upright.

"Shit," I whispered. "That's Stanton. I need . . . I have to . . ."

"Just sit tight for a second." He guided me back so I was sitting against the desk. Then he reached over me and lifted the phone off the hook. "CFAO White Beach Security, MA1 Gutiérrez, how may I help you, Sir or Ma'am?"

I didn't hear Stanton's voice. I felt it. It seemed to vibrate through the floor, across the desk, down from the walls, straight through my skin, and right to the bone.

"I understand, Sir," Gutiérrez said. "I needed her to take care of an urgent— Understood, Sir. I'm sorry, Sir. Yes, Sir. She'll be on her way in a moment, Sir." Lieutenant Stanton snarled something and then went silent. A second later, Gutiérrez rolled his eyes and hung up the phone. "Jesus."

I let my head fall back against the desk. "I'm so fucked."

Great choice of words, Kim. Real cute.

Gutiérrez touched my arm again. "Do you need someone to go in there with you?"

Please. Please don't make me do this alone.

But Stanton would kick him out in a heartbeat, and I didn't have the balls to explain why I couldn't face the Lieutenant by myself. I shook my head slowly. "No. I . . . I have to talk to him." My eyes flicked toward the trash can. "Fuck. I should—"

"I'll take care of that." Gutiérrez helped me to my feet. "Give yourself a minute if you need to." He nodded past me in the general direction of the ladies' room across the hall. "I'll get this squared away."

"Thanks." I forced a smile. His didn't look much more genuine.

I went into the restroom and splashed some water on my face. My eyes were still a little red, and my makeup was jacked up, but there wasn't much I could do about that, so I straightened my uniform and headed for Stanton's office.

On the way there, I clenched my jaw. There couldn't be much left in my stomach, but the nausea was back in full force. As long as Stanton was in the building, my guts would be on a hair trigger. It had been that way for the last week or two. No wonder the rumors were flying. One mad dash to the bathroom with a hand clapped over my mouth could be blamed on some ill-advised food or getting used to a foreign country's cuisine. Maybe some hard drinking the night before. The guys got away with it, anyway.

A second sprint, especially if it happened before noon, wasn't so easily explained.

And when a female third-class petty officer got called into the security officer's office *right now* in between bouts of incriminating puking?

Yeah. *That* wouldn't pour gas on the fire.

As I turned the corner at the end of the hall, I fought back tears as much as queasiness. By now, the names would be circulating. The boat ho without a boat. The shore-duty whore. The home-wrecking slut.

I paused outside Stanton's door and wiped my eyes. None of them had a goddamned clue. None of them. Not even Gutiérrez.

I took another deep breath. I straightened my police belt again, just for something to do. Tugged at my blue digicam blouse. Pretended it wasn't getting conspicuously tight on top.

And knocked.

I expected a terse, *Come in.*

Instead, the door opened, and . . .

And I was face-to-face with him.

Not Lieutenant Stanton, though.

Oh, sure, that was what the uniform said. The bars and ribbons, the gold insignia and the black lacquered name tag—to anyone else on the base, he was Lieutenant Stanton, Security Officer at Naval Station White Beach. The SECO, as we all called him. The man who answered to no one except the CO himself.

But the guy staring me down from six foot two with an expression carved in granite, he was someone I'd never met before. He wasn't the SECO, and he wasn't the bourbon-scented *Call me Joel* that had gotten me into this mess. This man was someone else entirely, and he scared the hell out of me.

He stood aside and jerked his head toward the office.

Every instinct I had screamed to run like hell, but he was a man with a long reach. If I ran away now, I'd have to come back sooner or later.

Don't run from the police, my uncle had always joked when we'd watched *Cops* years ago. *You'll only go to jail tired.*

I was tired enough. I was fucking exhausted.

So I didn't run.

I lowered my gaze, and I walked past him into the tiny room. The air conditioner and the concrete walls kept the office cold enough to make me wish my sleeves weren't rolled to just above my elbows. Goose bumps prickled my barearms, and the rest of my uniform—blue camouflage from neck to boot tops—did nothing to keep me warm.

Blinds cut across the window on the far side of the room, each hair-thin line emphasizing that the tropical paradise beyond was out of my reach. Palm trees fluttered in the wind, and at the other end of the parking lot and across the street, the turquoise water of Buckner Bay sparkled beside the White Beach pier. It was hot and humid out there, and just knowing that made me even colder.

The harbor-security boat bobbed on the waves, and I wished I'd taken the guys up on training out there today. The nausea wouldn't have been as bad. I had damned good sea legs, and anyway, I'd have been out there instead of in here.

In here with *him*.

The man who made acid sting the back of my throat as he silently walked past me. We faced each other. He leaned against his desk, our eyes almost level now as his posture brought him down to my height. Slowly, he folded his arms, and I wondered if it was deliberate, the way he put his left hand on top of his right arm so his wedding ring caught the light.

I squared my shoulders. "You wanted to see me, Sir?"

He held my gaze. "When were you going to tell me?"

There was no point in being coy. I pulled in a breath. "I don't know, Sir."

An odd smile quirked his lips. "You don't have to call me that right now, Kim. This is off the record. Personal."

Apparently there *was* something left in my stomach, but I swallowed just in time to put it back where it belonged. God, he was almost *Call me Joel* again.

The smile lingered as he rose to his full height. He came toward me, but as he reached for my arm, I jerked it away.

The smile vanished. Instantly. The Mr. Hyde part of him was back, hardening his features and narrowing his eyes. "Kim, we—"

"MA3 Lockhoff," I snapped. I was shivering from the inside out now. "Sir."

His lips pulled into a thin line, and he withdrew his hand. "This is a serious . . . situation."

"I know."

Our eyes locked for a long moment. Then he was back to Dr. Jekyll, his face relaxing a little. The sociopath was gone for now. "I would have liked it if we could have taken care of the problem before people started catching on, but there's—"

"Taken care of it?" I stared up at him.

He blinked. "Don't tell me you were planning on keeping it."

The truth was, I hadn't planned on much of anything. I'd only known for the past few days. Suspected it for maybe ten. Been fucking scared to death and deep in denial for the last seven and a half weeks. Not that I'd been counting.

Planning? Future? None of that had even registered yet.

"I'm not aborting it." I fucking *hated* how timid I sounded just then.

"Are you an idiot?" *Welcome back, Mr. Hyde.* He threw up his hands. "Kim, think about—"

"My name is MA3 Lockhoff." My voice tried to break, but I kept it steady. Sort of. "*Sir.*"

He eyed me coolly. "Fine. MA3 Lockhoff." He closed the distance between us, standing so close he could have touched me, but he didn't. "Get it taken care of."

And what if I don't? I wanted to ask. *What are you going to do? Order me to get an abortion?*

But fear kept the air in my lungs and the words between my tightly clenched teeth. I broke our staring contest to blink—once, twice, again—and to keep him from seeing the tears that threatened.

They're just hormones. I'm not afraid of him.

I am not *afraid of him.*

Yeah, right.

Little by little, his expression softened. "No one's going to care. Girls in the Navy do it all the time." He brought up his hand and touched my cheek. I wanted to bat away his warm, sickening caress, but I was paralyzed. "Rumors will spread, but as long as the problem goes away, people will forget about it. No one has to know the details." The slight arch of his eyebrow emphasized the last part, and something so subtle had never been that menacing before.

No one will know the details, his eyes warned. *Will they?*

I gulped. *No, Sir.*

Because it's going to be taken care of, isn't it?

Yes, Sir.

"I want it done discreetly. Preferably off-island." He trailed his hand down my cheek, then over my jaw. As it went lower, the touch slowly became a grasp, his thumb across my windpipe and his long fingers around the side and back of my neck. "Drop a leave chit ASAP. Take a week. Two, if you need it. I'll make sure the leave is approved." His thumb ran up and down the front of my throat. "There are flights out of Kadena to Hawaii twice a week. Or go back to the States. I don't care. Just"—another slow down-up—"get it done."

I cleared my throat, which pushed it against his thumb. "Yes, Sir."

He smiled. Really smiled. *Call me Joel* smiled. His hand left my neck and went back up to my face, and the other one cupped my other cheek. "Take my advice and everything will be okay, Kim. Don't worry about a thing."

He leaned in like he was about to kiss me, but I stopped him with a hand to his chest and turned my head. I could feel the sudden rage in his posture, so I quickly murmured, "I was . . . sick. Before I came in here."

That gave him pause. He settled on kissing my forehead, which was marginally less nauseating than a full-on kiss.

Then, thank God, he drew back. "I'll expect that leave chit on your LPO's desk first thing in the morning."

"Yes, Sir."

CHAPTER 2
REESE

I stepped into the precinct and exhaled as the cold air hit my face. The air-conditioning in my patrol car was broken, so walking into this place was a huge relief. Even if I didn't feel like handling whatever bullshit my boss had called me in off patrol to deal with, it got me out of the heat and humidity for a little while.

MA3 Weiss, my partner, fanned himself with his cover. "Man, it's too fucking hot out there, but I'm going to go have a smoke."

"Go for it. I'll be out as soon as I'm done with whatever MA1 wants."

"Good luck."

"Thanks."

"That was fast, MA2," Alejandro—MA1 Gutiérrez to everyone else—said as he stepped into the room.

I shrugged and dropped my cover on the communal desk. "We were just up by the gate. Not too—" I paused when I noticed the wastebasket in his hand and watched him set it down. "Chief's got you on trash detail, boss man?"

He smirked, but it quickly faded. He toed the wastebasket closer to the desk, as if he wanted it as far away from himself as possible. "Listen, uh . . . I need a favor."

Oh, for fuck's sake. Another one? Feigning infinite patience, I smiled. "What do you need?"

He glanced over his shoulder at the door leading to the hallway. When he faced me again, he lowered his chin and his voice and said, "It's about MA3 Lockhoff."

Forget faking patience. I groaned. "Now what?"

Usually, he'd have chuckled. He knew how much I hated being the go-to girl when other females in the command couldn't get their shit together in this male-dominated environment. For some reason, he expected me to be the mother hen for all these chicks. Specifically, the mother hen who'd grab wayward girls by the hair, dunk their faces in a nice bucket of reality, and teach them how not to set gender equality back ten years every time they opened their goddamned mouths. Or legs, as it were.

Alejandro always thought it was entertaining as hell, watching me straighten out girls who had no business in the Navy, never mind as cops. Especially when the girl in question was a vapid twit like MA3 Lockhoff. The kind who used her pretty little smile and her pretty not-so-little tits to bend every man on the island to her cute little will. MA3 Lockhoff was one of the reasons we got emails before every formal event reminding the female service members to *please* not dress like whores this time. Women like her drove me insane, and Alejandro lived to watch them do it.

Today, though, he wasn't joking. The tension in his neck and between his eyebrows hadn't been there this morning, and he only pressed his lips together like that when he was deathly serious.

I cocked my head. "What's going on?"

He hesitated, then gestured for me to follow him. We stepped across the hall into the office he shared with MA1 Harris, who wasn't there, and he shut the door.

"Alejandro, what's going on?" I practically whispered it, and not just because I didn't want anyone hearing us on a first name basis.

He cradled his elbow in his hand and chewed his other thumbnail. "You've, uh, probably heard the rumors, right?"

"Which ones?" I struggled to keep the sarcasm out of my voice. "Rumors have been going around like crazy ever since she checked in." She'd been at the command for six months, and I was pretty sure she'd fucked her way through the barracks, a couple of off-base apartments, and the temporary lodging on both the White Beach and Kadena bases for good measure.

"Yeah, well." He exhaled hard. "She got sick during PT yesterday. And at a meeting the other day. And"—he gestured back at the office we'd just left—"today."

"Got 'sick'? As in . . ."

He nodded.

I covered my face with one hand. "Oh Christ. Please tell me she just can't deal with the heat."

"Afraid not."

"Fuck."

"It gets better."

I looked at him through my fingers.

He rubbed the back of his neck. "Were you at Senior Chief O'Leary's retirement?"

I wrinkled my nose and dropped my hand. "Unfortunately. I don't think I'll ever get the taste of his wife's potato salad out of my mouth."

No humor. Not even the faintest laugh. Jesus. What the hell was going on?

Alejandro swallowed. "She was, uh, flirting. With a lot of the guys."

"That's news," I muttered.

Still nothing.

Alejandro lowered his gaze, and his voice was barely audible. "I saw her leave with Lieutenant Stanton."

My heart stopped. "Oh my God. Stanton? Really? Didn't he have his wife with him that night?"

He shook his head. "Not that time. I think she was off-island. Or something. I don't know. But I saw him and MA3 getting a little, uh, cozy, and the—"

"And no one said anything?" I huffed sharply. "He's *how* many pay grades above her?"

"And they're both of age," Alejandro snapped. "Remember, every goddamned person at that barbecue wanted to make rank eventually. You really think any of us were getting between him and a piece-of-ass du jour?"

I said nothing. Wouldn't I have done the same thing if I'd seen them? Of course I would have. If I didn't get promoted in the next couple of cycles, my Navy career was over, so stepping in between two consenting adults—even if they were drunk off their asses, which I had no doubt they were—when it meant career suicide? Not a chance.

"So what do you want me to do?" I asked. "That was weeks ago."

"Yeah." He looked me straight in the eyes. "About, oh, not quite eight weeks ago." He gestured at the door again. "And now MA3's getting sick all over the office."

The pieces came together in my head.

"Oh God." I put a hand over my mouth. "Oh my God."

"Yeah." He ran his fingers through his short hair. "She's in his office right now. He called her in right before I called you. And he is *not* happy."

"I don't imagine he is. His wife is going to skin him alive."

"I'm a little worried about her, to be honest. Lockhoff, I mean."

I raised an eyebrow. "Why?"

"She was a mess." He grimaced. "Not just because she was sick. I mean, she was fine this afternoon right up until Stanton came into the precinct. Quieter than usual, but fine. Then he shows up, tells her to come into his office, and suddenly she's shaking like a leaf."

"Wouldn't you be?" I shrugged and folded my arms across my blouse. "If I had to tell Stanton I was having his kid, I'd be a wreck, too, and not just because I'd let that creep put his dick in me."

He *still* didn't laugh. "Listen, I know I'm always asking you to help the new girls get their shit straight, but this time, I think she really needs someone."

"Alejandro . . ."

"Please." He spoke even softer now. "I might be imagining things, but my gut feeling is she could really use some support right now."

I pressed the tip of my tongue to the roof of my mouth, fighting the urge to roll my eyes again. "You want me to support her? When she's gotten herself into a stupid situation like that?" I shook my head. "You know damn well I'm liable to tell her how it is and make her cry. I can't even put up with the other girls using their periods to get out of PT. You really think I'm the best person for this?"

"I can't think of anyone else, Reese," he whispered. "I know you don't have any patience for girls getting themselves into shit situations, but you've got your head together and your feet on the ground. Just . . . talk to her. Make sure she's all right and let her know you're there if she needs you."

"And what am I supposed to say if she wants my sympathy for getting into this mess?"

Alejandro blew out a breath. "If I knew, I'd do it myself. Right now, it's all I can do not to drag her in here and chew her out for being stupid enough to have an affair with a higher-up. That kid's going to fuck both of their careers, especially Stanton's."

I pursed my lips. Alejandro liked Lieutenant Stanton a hell of a lot more than I did, but I wasn't about to get into another argument with him about the man's lack of virtue.

One thing we did agree on, though, was that girls like MA3 Lockhoff were part of the reason women in the military still didn't get the respect we deserved.

But whether Alejandro and I agreed with her choices or not, she was still his Sailor. She was technically *my* Sailor, since I outranked her. And rank aside, she was a fellow cop. For that matter, as geographically isolated as we were on this island, people had no choice but to rely on their command for support because friends, families, and civilian resources were an ocean away from all of us.

I didn't have to agree with what she did, but I couldn't throw her to the wolves, either.

Swearing under my breath, I rubbed my eyes with my thumb and forefinger. Then I dropped my hand and glared at him. "You owe me so big for this."

And finally—*finally*—he smiled. "Thank you."

"I need a cigarette," I muttered.

Usually that would have elicited an ironic *Those things will kill you, you know* comment from him, but he'd already pulled a can of dip out of his back pocket and would probably have a pinch of it tucked into his cheek before we made it out the door. Lucky bastard.

We left his office and headed back toward the communal one, but before I could get outside to smoke, someone out in the hall said, "You okay, MA3?"

Alejandro and I both stiffened and turned to each other.

"I'm fine." Even from here, Lockhoff sounded anything but fine.

Alejandro glanced at me, eyebrows up in an unspoken *Please don't bail on me*. I gave a slight nod, and he relaxed a little.

A second later, she stepped into the front office.

And good God, she looked like hell.

Her uniform was squared away as always, and she'd pulled her near-black hair back into a tight bun, but she was paler than anyone on a tropical island had a right to be. Her eyeliner wasn't as perfect and smoky as it usually was. I suspected that had something to do with the redness in her eyes.

She stopped in the doorway, her cover in both hands. Her eyes flicked back and forth between me and Alejandro.

"How'd it go?" he asked quietly.

She glanced at me again, eyes narrowing as if to say, *A little privacy, please?*

Don't mind if I do.

I put on my cover and made a beeline for the door. "I'm going to have a smoke."

Alejandro nodded but didn't look at me.

As I stepped out, I'd never been so grateful for that rush of tropical heat. In ten minutes, I'd be praying for sweet death and looking for any reason to either step into an air-conditioned building or strip out of this suffocating blouse and heavy police belt, but for the moment I basked in it.

I went up to the smoke pit—a gazebo twenty meters from the precinct with a couple of chairs and a coffee-can ashtray. There, I lit a cigarette and took a deep drag. As the nicotine seeped into my bloodstream, some of the tightness in my shoulders unwound. I rolled them slowly and replayed my conversation with Alejandro.

I loved the man to death, but it drove me crazy the way he believed I was the one who should handle situations like this. If it was because she was a junior Sailor and it was my damned responsibility, fine. But he and I both knew that wasn't the case. Alejandro hadn't called on me when some idiot seaman had been caught having an ill-advised affair with Senior Chief Ellis's wife or last year when one kid's drinking problem had gotten out of control and almost caused an international incident.

But when a woman who'd gotten on my nerves since the day she'd checked in decided to get herself into a situation like this? Suddenly he was speed-dialing MA2 Marion, the female- Sailor whisperer. As if my tits and ovaries made me more qualified than anyone else—including her *boss*, damn it—to tell Lockhoff she was being stupid.

I rolled my eyes and blew out some smoke.

Truth be told, I had hoped Lockhoff wasn't that kind of girl. I'd been disappointed as fuck when I realized she was, well, her, because on the surface, she was very much my type. She had the fit physique that the military demanded, but there was also something about the way she carried herself that made my heart race. Chin up, shoulders back, looking the world in the eye. And the few times I'd seen her in civvies with minimal makeup and that dark hair falling down, she'd been . . . Hell, who was I kidding? She was stunning.

Maybe that was why she irritated me so much. She was everything I wanted physically in a woman, and she was everything *else* that made my teeth grind.

The door opened a few minutes later, and Lockhoff came out and joined me in the smoke pit. She'd taken off her police belt and downloaded—no gun, no pepper spray. While I finished my cigarette, she stared off into the distance and eventually broke the silence. "Listen, um, Gutiérrez wants me to go over to Camp Courtney. To medical. He said you were heading that way." After a moment, she met my eyes. "Would you mind giving me a lift?"

Alejandro, you bastard . . .

I dropped my cigarette and crushed it under the toe of my boot. "Sure. Let's go."

I poked my head into dispatch to let Weiss know I had to run an errand for Gutiérrez, and then Lockhoff and I walked across the parking lot to my patrol car.

"The AC's busted." I rolled down my window. "Sorry."

"Does it work in any of the vehicles?" she muttered and rolled hers down, too.

"Not really. Just the one Stanton drives around."

I wasn't sure, but I thought she shuddered.

In silence, I drove us through the gate and out onto the main road. At least now that we were off-base, I could drive faster. Twenty clicks an hour didn't generate much of a cross breeze in the car, but fifty plus did the trick, and after a few minutes, the air was nice and cool.

Beside me, Lockhoff stared out the window.

"So, um." I cleared my throat. "You okay? You seem a little . . ."

Pregnant with Stanton's kid? Yeah, that would be tactful.

"I'm fine." She didn't look at me.

"Okay. Uh . . ." I idly played with the peeling cover on the wheel. "Well, Gutiérrez wanted me to take you to medical. Do you need me to stick around to give you a ride back after?"

"You don't mind?"

"Just doing what Gutiérrez asked."

"Oh. Okay. Yeah, I do need a ride back. Thanks." She was quiet for a moment, then finally turned to me. "Do you mind if I ask you something? That doesn't leave this car?"

That question was a dangerous one when it came from the woman carrying our married superior's kid, but I managed to unstick my tongue from the roof of my mouth and give a quiet, "Go ahead."

She didn't say a word for almost a full minute, instead just staring straight ahead, a hand on her stomach right above her seat belt. I wondered if she hadn't heard me and was still waiting for permission to ask, but then she said, "How confidential is a sexual assault report?"

I damn near ran off the road. "What?"

Lockhoff squirmed in the passenger seat. "If I wanted to talk . . . If someone wanted to talk to the SARC, is it confidential? Or an official report?"

You want to talk to the Sexual Assault Response Coordinator? About . . .

Seriously?

I will fucking choke her. Pull this goddamned car over, fly into the passenger seat, and fucking choke her. Sexual assault?

Oh hell no, sweetie. Half the command saw you leave with Lieutenant Stanton. No way they would've stood by and let him drag you out against your will.

Gripping the wheel tighter, I focused on the road. Women like her didn't just give the rest of us a bad name. They were the reason the real sexual assaults weren't taken seriously.

It's sexual assault when you wake up tasting blood. Not when he doesn't want to leave his wife and raise your kid, you little bitch.

"I'm not sure." I forced myself to speak evenly. "I've never needed to . . . I've never reported one."

Silence fell. I didn't realize she'd been staring at me until I glanced at her again.

Her tone was flat when she finally spoke. "You don't believe me."

Not even a little.

"I don't know the details."

"But you've already made up your mind, haven't you?" She kept her voice low and calm, but the slightest waver gave me pause.

"I . . ." I didn't have an answer. Not one that would've gone down easily, anyway.

"Stop the car."

"What?"

"Just stop. I'll get a cab to medical."

"I didn't say I didn't believe you, MA3." *But you don't, do you?* "I—"

"Stop the fucking car," she hissed.

What else could I do?

I pulled the patrol car up to the curb. "MA3, listen. We—"

But she was gone.

Fuck. Gutiérrez would have my head on a stake if this got back to him.

And if she really had been assaulted, then . . .

Damn it.

She was right: I didn't believe her.

But . . .

I had nothing to base my disbelief on except her reputation, which would mean buying into the nauseating motto some of the guys on my last deployment had lived by: *You can't rape the willing.*

But how could I assume she *had* been willing? Eagerly fucking ten men in a row didn't mean she was obligated to fuck the eleventh, or that it wasn't rape if he fucked her anyway.

And I'd *sworn* that no matter how much some of the pretty girls drove me insane, I'd take every sexual assault report seriously. From any woman. Any man, too. Any cop gave them grief, I'd have them hemmed up so fast their heads would spin. I, of all people, had no business sandbagging a woman who'd worked up the courage to report an assault. Especially against a superior.

And now . . . this?

My mouth went dry as she strode farther away.

Every cop needed a sixth sense about these things, and Alejandro's was better than any I'd ever known. His gut had told him this situation was off enough to warrant bringing in a woman to offer her some support, so maybe he'd caught onto something I'd missed.

Whatever the case, what right did I have to decide if Lockhoff had or hadn't been raped?

There was no legitimate reason for her to be storming off alone in the blistering heat after Alejandro had tasked me with making sure she was all right.

Jesus Christ. What did I just do?

I quickly shifted into drive and peeled away from the curb. As I pulled up beside her, I slowed down again and called out the window, "MA3, wait."

She didn't stop.

"Please, just get in the car."

She spun on her heel and faced me, and I hit the brake. She leaned on the open window and glared at me. "Why? So you can—"

I put up my hand. "Listen, I'm sorry. I . . . Can we please go sit down somewhere and talk?"

Her eyes narrowed. "Why don't you just pull rank and order me?"

I gritted my teeth. "Get in the car, MA3."

She muttered something under her breath, probably something that amounted to gross insubordination, but I let it go. I deserved it.

And at least she got back in the car.

CHAPTER 3
KIM

MA2 Marion drove us onto Camp Courtney, and we walked into the tiny food court near the gate. She waited in line to order us a couple of bottles of water from the Burger King while I snagged a corner table.

As I watched her, my stomach was still doing somersaults. I didn't trust anyone at this command. It shouldn't have surprised me that I didn't have an ally in her. Hell, the first moment I'd set foot in the precinct, she'd looked me up and down, and she hadn't quite turned her head before she'd rolled her eyes in that *Oh Lord, she's one of those* kind of way.

I wanted to like her. Hell, I'd had a crush on her from the start—bitch or not, she was *gorgeous*. And more than that, she was a take-no-shit cop and a squared-away Sailor. Exactly the kind of cop and Sailor I wanted to be. My first thought, after noticing how her uniform fit, was that I wanted her as a mentor, but she obviously didn't like me. I wasn't sure if she liked anyone, actually. MA1 Gutiérrez, maybe, since they obviously had something going on. Otherwise, Marion pretty much kept to herself and didn't speak unless spoken to.

It didn't surprise me when I'd heard she'd been over to Afghanistan and maybe Iraq. A lot of people came back from the Sandbox with a distinct look about them. Like part of them was still over there, and the part that had come back had . . . dimmed.

But I'd thought if there was anyone in the command who I could tip my hand to, it was her. She was a woman, after all. Every woman in the military knew the risk we took just by enlisting. The other female in our command worked nights, so we never crossed paths, plus she was also barely out of boot camp. She had almost no experience being out of high school, never mind with some of the harsher realities of military life—I hoped, anyway. For her own sake.

MA2 Marion had been in for several years, though, and she'd been to a couple of war zones, so she had to know how often this shit happened.

Yet her first instinct had been skepticism. Hostile skepticism. Even if she hadn't said it out loud, I'd seen it in the way her jaw had tightened and her eyes had narrowed.

I tore my gaze away and stared down at the table, wringing my sweaty hands. I didn't have to ask what was going through her mind. She and everyone else on this island thought the same thing about girls like me. That was why I'd never reported it to begin with. Why I probably still wouldn't. Why I was desperately searching for a reason to avoid going to medical like MA1 Gutiérrez had ordered me to.

My heart sank, and I sagged back against the cold metal chair. I didn't have many options, did I? And either way, even if I reported it, I was still pregnant. For now, at least.

"Just get it done."

I shuddered.

"You all right?"

Marion's voice startled me. I looked up as she joined me at the table with two water bottles in hand.

"I'm fine." I took one of the bottles she'd offered. "Thanks."

"Don't mention it." She avoided my eyes for a moment, then cleared her throat as she unscrewed the cap on her bottle. "Look, I'm sorry. I didn't mean—"

"If you don't believe me, you don't believe me."

"It's not that simple."

"You didn't believe me in the car."

MA2 Marion's shoulders fell. "I . . . Listen, I just wasn't expecting it, that's all. I'm sorry."

I chewed my lip. "Most women would err on the side of finding out what the fuck happened before they pass judgment."

"You're absolutely right. And I've been kicking myself ever since." She finally met my eyes, and her expression was softer than I'd ever seen it. "I meant it when I apologized, and I mean it when I tell you this stays between you and me, I promise. Just tell me what happened."

"I . . ." Of course my subconscious chose that moment to kick in and remind me of the gleaming gold shield on her uniform. My gaze shifted to the badge, and my heart dropped.

Anyone else on this island could listen to me in confidence.

But not her. Not a mandated reporter.

I exhaled. "It can't stay between us. You're a cop. I'm a cop. If I tell you something happened, then you have to report it."

Marion swallowed. "Except you've already basically told me that *something* happened."

"But I haven't said what."

She held my gaze. Yeah, she knew. Of course she did. But woman's intuition wasn't evidence.

Marion swore and sat back. "Fuck..."

I played with the cap on my water bottle. Even if her first instinct had been to disbelieve me, and even if she was a mandated reporter, who else *could* I talk to? Of course, I could tell her and ask her to keep it quiet, but then if it came out later that she knew, she'd be screwed.

She drummed her fingers beside her water bottle. "Do you want me to take you over to see the SARC?"

I shook my head. "I don't know. I'm ... kind of not sure who I can trust." I arched an eyebrow. "Doesn't seem like many people take me seriously." I exhaled and rolled some tightness out of my shoulders. "I mean, what should I do? I don't know if I can talk to the SARC."

"This is his job, though. If you can't trust the SARC, then ..." She sighed and lowered her gaze. "I get it. I do. Commands like this are so incestuous, it's hard to know who to trust." Through her teeth, she added, "Assuming there's anyone you *can* trust."

I swallowed, not sure if I was relieved that she didn't think I was crazy or if I wanted to cry because she'd confirmed one of my biggest fears. Probably a little of both.

I took a drink just to wet my mouth. Then, "I don't know if I'm going to report anything or not. I ... I need to think on it."

"MA3, if he ..." She chewed her lip. "If something happened, you need to report it or nothing can be done."

"And what do you think *can* be done?" I narrowed my eyes. "You really think an E4 who the whole command thinks is a slut is going to convince anybody of anything?"

She dropped her gaze, and my stomach twisted into knots. Nothing like having more of my worst fears—and that asshole's threats—confirmed. By another woman, no less.

"You still need to go to medical." She continued avoiding my eyes. "So they can confirm, um . . . Well, so they can get you a light duty chit, for one thing."

I cringed. So she knew, too. Then again, I supposed most people knew by now, especially cops who were trained to be observant. Shifting me to light duty wouldn't help with the rumors flying around. But of course, unless I did what Stanton had ordered me to, I wouldn't be able to hide this much longer. Sooner or later, I'd have to break down and switch to a maternity uniform, but I wasn't ready to announce anything to the universe. Especially not to all the assholes who'd been taking bets on who'd knock me up first.

Watching Marion shift uncomfortably, I wondered if she'd won or lost money in that betting pool.

She sat up straighter and folded her arms on the table. "Listen, let's get you over to medical. Make sure you're taken care of." She met my eyes. "If you decide you want to make a statement, or you need someone to go to the SARC with you, let me know."

I nodded. "If I go to medical, they're automatically going to give me a light duty chit, aren't they?"

"Probably, yeah."

"Shit."

Marion furrowed her brow. "Why?"

"Where do they send most MAs on light duty? Either Pass & ID, training, or dispatch." I swallowed hard to keep what was left in my stomach where it belonged. "Training or dispatch means working in the same building as Stanton."

"Oh. Shit." She grimaced. "Well, I'm sure Gutiérrez could pull some strings."

"And if he can't?"

She broke eye contact and slowly shook her head. "I don't know."

"Maybe I should wait." I took a deep breath. "At least sleep on it."

She met my gaze again.

"Please," I whispered, cursing the pitiful sound of my own voice. "I'm not ready to be penned up in the same building with him. And my shift's almost over today anyway. It's not like I'll be out on any calls."

"But tomorrow . . ."

"I'll figure it out. Just . . . not now."

"But you're . . ." She held my gaze and then sighed. "Okay. It's your call. But when you're ready, let me know."

"I will. Thanks."

"And . . ." She bit her lip, dropping her gaze for a second. "I'm sorry. For not . . ."

I capped my water bottle. "Don't worry about. We, uh . . ." I glanced at the clock on the wall. "We should get back to White Beach since we're not going to medical."

She nodded. "Okay. Let's go."

"Hey, Lockhoff." Barkley gestured over his shoulder on his way into the front office the next morning. "Stanton wants to see you."

I shuddered hard, my toes curling inside my boots. It had been less than twenty-four hours since the last time I'd stepped into Stanton's office. My stomach and I were nowhere near ready for another face-to-face with him, but the sooner I got it over with, the sooner I could go puke in peace.

"Thanks." I closed the logbook and got up from the desk. There was no point in trying to prepare myself because there was no preparing to face that bastard. Once I was sure my breakfast would stay down long enough for me to get to the end of the hall, I went straight to his office and knocked.

He didn't greet me at the door this time, and the terse "It's open" made my stomach turn. I took a deep breath and let myself in.

He didn't look up. "Close the door."

I hesitated. Privacy was fine and good, but I wasn't sure how I felt about being confined in a room with him again. Blood pounded in my ears as I toed the door shut.

I stood between the desk and doorway, not quite at attention or parade rest, but still rigid and straight with my hands behind my back. For a long, unnerving moment, Stanton didn't even look at me. He continued whatever he'd been working on, perusing some forms and paperwork, signing a couple of things, and shuffling them around like business as usual.

I forced myself to keep my face as neutral as I could. Whatever head game this was—*You're lower on my priority list than this paperwork. Everything we do is at my whim. Your presence doesn't fuck with me like I know mine fucks with you*—I wasn't playing it. Instead, I concentrated on not locking my knees and not vomiting on his paperwork.

Finally, he closed the file folder. In what seemed like a deliberately slow motion, he capped his pen and set it in the brass cup on his desk. Then and *only* then, he lifted his gaze.

The clock above the door behind me marked time with quiet clicks that seemed to echo in the otherwise silent office. He stared up at me. I stared down at him. Was he trying to intimidate me? Fuck with me? *Too bad, asshole.*

Instead of trying to guess his next move, I searched his face for some scrap of the man who'd charmed me out of that party and into his car. Nowhere in those stony features did I see *Call me Joel* this time. I'd seen flickers of this side of him before, though. That night, the stark light from the streetlamps had made the shadows deeper, sharpened every angle and darkened his eyes. I couldn't put my finger on exactly how his expression had changed, only that there had been a moment when I'd been staring up at him, and between his fierce grip on my arms and *that look*, the message had come through loud and clear:

This is happening. The only choice you have right now is how much it hurts.

Even now, in the softer fluorescent light, his face was enough to make me want to recoil.

I swallowed hard, forcing the contents of my stomach to stay where they were, and then cleared my throat. "You wanted to see me, Sir?"

Stanton smiled thinly, and the unspoken threat still lingered in his eyes. Slowly, he stood. As he came around the desk, I was tempted to make a run for the door, but I planted my feet. He wasn't going to hurt me. Not here. There were people around. One scream, and this office would be full of cops. And we both knew I was trained to use the Taser, pepper spray, baton, and nine-millimeter on my belt.

No, I was not afraid of him.

Not at all.

Stanton stopped directly in front of me so we were toe-to-toe. The smile was gone, and he lifted his chin as he glared down at me.

I gulped and managed to repeat, "You wanted to see me, Sir?"

"I haven't seen a leave chit." He folded his arms across his chest, ribbons and insignia crunching quietly beneath them. "And don't tell me it's on MA1 Gutiérrez's desk or that Chief Wolcott has it. I've already checked."

My blood turned cold. He checked with them? How much did they know? Besides the fact that he had suddenly taken an interest in a third-class petty officer's leave chit?

I took a deep breath. "I haven't routed the chit, Sir."

"Why not?"

"Because I don't know what I'm going to do yet."

"You don't—" His eyes narrowed, and ice formed along my veins as he growled, "What do you mean, you don't know? Get it *done*, MA3."

"With all due respect," I hissed, "this isn't your decision to make." I clenched my teeth. "*Sir.*"

He leaned in closer, his face just inches from mine. "On the contrary, MA3. I'm in this situation as much as—"

"You chose to put us both in this situation."

His eyebrows jumped. "Took two to tango, my dear."

"You *raped* me." I was genuinely stunned when the floor didn't fall out from under us after the words came out. After I looked him straight in the eye and said them. But it didn't, and we were still standing there, and the rage burning in his eyes was quickly reducing me to the girl who'd let herself be fucked in the passenger seat of his car. There wasn't a weapon on my belt that could shield me from his fury.

"Raped you?" he snarled. "The hell I did. We both know you wanted it just as much as—"

"The hell *I* did."

He laughed dryly. "You think you're going to convince a jury? Because I can bring in a dozen character witnesses who'll testify as to what kind of woman you are, MA3, and how much you'd had to drink that night." He cupped my chin roughly, forcing me to look him in the eyes. "And just in case you have any ideas about pressing charges like a goddamned idiot, I promise you that when I'm found not guilty, which I will be, I'll expect to be able to see my kid."

"What?" I managed a humorless laugh because it was that or a terrified sob. "One second you want me to abort this baby. The next you want visitation?"

"No, I don't want visitation. I don't want anything to do with this kid because I want you to do the smart fucking thing and get rid of it. But if you're going to be fucking stupid, then let me spell this out for you." He loomed over me. "If you don't get the abortion and you press charges against me, then you're admitting I'm the father of your kid."

I swallowed and jerked my chin out of his hand.

He came closer, pushing me back against the door with his sheer presence. "If I'm the father, then I have paternal rights. And I *promise* you, if you try to nuke my life and career with this kid and this 'rape' bullshit, I will exercise every last one of those rights."

I just stared at him. Couldn't speak.Couldn't breathe.

"If you try to pull this stunt, the only thing you're going to regret more than carrying that kid to term is accusing me of raping you." He leaned in, his breath hot on my face. "So I would suggest you let this go and get your ass off this island and into a clinic."

"You and I both—" My voice cracked, and I coughed before I went on. "You and I both know what it was that night. The SARC will believe—"

"The SARC?" He smirked. "You mean Bill Jackson? Who my wife and I had dinner with the other night and I played golf with just this past weekend?"

My heart dropped.

"That's right, MA3. And you might be interested to know about the conversation we had out on the green." His expression hardened. "Seems that false accusations of sexual assault can do a number on a young lady's career."

The space between us shrank to almost nothing, and I pressed myself up against the door as hard as I could as he spoke through his teeth. "Bill believes very much in prosecuting sexual assaults. He takes them *very* seriously." Stanton put a heavy hand on my shoulder. "And he also believes that false accusations are—"

"It's not a false accusation and you know it."

His eyes narrowed, and his hand was somehow even heavier. "Just because you regret it after the fact because I knocked you up doesn't mean it was assault."

I laughed bitterly and shrugged his hand away, though the door behind my back kept me from escaping completely. "You know what happened."

"And so do you. Now do we have an understanding?"

I didn't respond. I couldn't. I refused to believe he'd backed me against a metaphorical wall as well as the physical one.

"Do we have an understanding, MA3?"

I gritted my teeth. "Yes, Sir."

"Good." He took a step back, which allowed me to release my breath. "I'll expect your leave chit before the end of the day. And if you get it done on-island, at least use a little common sense and get it done off-base. So there's no record and no question."

"I can't . . ." I stood straighter. "I can't afford something like that."

"I figured you couldn't. All the more reason to get it done, am I right, MA3?" He sneered. "If you can't afford to get rid of it, you can't afford to keep it, either." He turned around and snatched something off his desk. He shoved it at me, and I took it without thinking. As soon as it was in my hand, I could tell exactly what it was by the weight and thickness—an envelope stuffed with cash. "That will cover it."

"You know how much an abortion costs off-base?"

Stanton glared at me, and I shrank back, phantom hands gripping my upper arms all over again.

"Get it done, MA3."

I clutched the envelope. "Yes, Sir."

"Dismissed."

I left his office and sprinted straight to the ladies' room.

When nothing else would come up, I sat back on my heels in the stall and wiped my mouth with a shaking hand. What the hell was I supposed to do now? Give in and move on? Stand up to him and risk him exercising his parental rights?

And on top of it all, for the millionth time since Senior Chief O'Leary's retirement party, the same question ran through my mind:

Did he rape me?

I wanted to believe he hadn't because I didn't want to believe that could happen to me. It was something that happened in sexual assault response-training anecdotes. It happened to people in other places. Millions of miles away. Not me. Not a cop. It didn't. It couldn't!

But I'd said no, and the sex had happened anyway.

Countless hours of law enforcement training echoed through my mind. All those catch phrases—*No means no. Rape doesn't have to be violent. Coercion counts*—meant nothing while I sat on a dirty bathroom floor, pregnant with the baby of a man I'd never have slept with voluntarily.

And what the hell did it matter anyway? He was friends with everyone in our incestuous, good ole boys chain of command. Including the Sexual Assault Response Coordinator. Who didn't tolerate girls making false accusations of rape. No matter what had really happened, the fact remained it was my word against Stanton's, and the word of a girl with a slutty reputation and only one chevron on her collar didn't carry much weight against a respected officer's.

I closed my eyes, my heart sinking as my stomach threatened to lurch again. My eyes stung, and I told myself it was from puking or hormones or anything besides the realization that I had no options here. No choice but to walk away from as much of this situation as I could and move on.

I forced myself to my feet, flushed the toilet, and went to the sink. I rinsed out my mouth and cleaned up my face, clearing away the muddy smears of mascara and eyeliner so I looked halfway presentable.

Hands on the edges of the sink, I met my own gaze in the mirror.

I know the truth. Even if he never goes down for it, he still has to sleep at night.

I know what happened, but I have to take care of myself.

Even if it means he walks away scot-free.

My eyes threatened to tear up again, and I dabbed at them with a paper towel. Then I took a few slow, deep breaths and ordered myself to get through this. Maybe Stanton would get away with what he did, and it would be up to karma to serve any justice, but he would *not* beat me down. This would *not* destroy me.

Once I was sure my composure wasn't going to fall apart, I left the ladies' room and headed down the hall to MA1 Gutiérrez's office.

His door was open, so I tapped my knuckle on the frame. "MA1?"

He looked up from his paperwork, and his expression stayed neutral as he set his pen down and folded his hands. "What can I do for you, MA3?"

"I, um . . ." I stepped into his office and shut the door behind me. "I need to put in a leave chit. If I route one today, can my leave start tomorrow?"

"Is it an emergency?"

Yes. Holy shit, yes. "No. But I . . . It's a personal matter. With all due respect, it's something I need to address and would rather not get into."

His eyebrows rose. I expected him to mention they were short on bodies, that staffing was difficult right now as it was without someone disappearing on a moment's notice, but he just said, "Do you have all the information? Flights? Hotel?"

"I'll be taking a Space-A flight. To Hawaii. I . . . haven't booked the hotel yet."

"It needs to be on the chit."

"I know." I locked eyes with him and gulped. "I'll . . . I'll work out all the details."

"How long do you need?"

"Probably ten days."

He steepled his fingers. "Give it to me in the next hour, and I'll make sure it's signed off by the end of the day." As he spoke, some tension melted out of his shoulders. He seemed to stop just short of breathing a sigh of relief, but I had a feeling that would happen as soon as I left his office.

Thanks, MA1. Nice to know whose side you're on here.

CHAPTER 4

REESE

Oh Christ. Now what?

In the passenger seat of the patrol car, I stared at my silent cell phone.

"What was that all about?" Weiss asked.

"That was Gutiérrez. He wants me to come back."

"Again?" He huffed sharply. "We haven't even made our rounds yet."

"Must be something important." I sipped my water to moisten my suddenly dry mouth. "Just take me back. Whatever it is, it probably won't take long."

"Does this mean I'm going to be stuck in dispatch while you're off running errands again?"

"Let's hope not."

While he turned the car around, I shoved my phone in my pocket and dug out my cigarettes and lighter.

"Want one?"

"I just had one. So did you."

I put a smoke between my lips. "Suit yourself."

In the time it took him to drive us from Camp Shields, where we'd been assigned for the day, back to White Beach, I went through two cigarettes. As he pulled up in front of the precinct, I was seriously considering a third. The only thing that stopped me was the fact that I was already creeping up on two and a half packs a day, and I refused to reach three.

We walked inside, and Weiss disappeared down the hall, probably so he could shoot the shit with whoever was working in dispatch.

Alejandro's door was open, so I walked straight into his office. "You wanted to see me?"

"Yes." He stood as I closed the door. "What did Lockhoff say yesterday?"

"Nothing yet."

"Nothing at all?"

I shook my head. *Don't make me betray her confidence, Alejandro. I'm already on thin ice with her.*

"But she did go to medical?"

"Um . . ."

His eyebrow arched. "I thought you were—"

"She opted not to go."

"What? Why?"

I glared at him. "You know I couldn't divulge anything medical even if I wanted to."

Not unless a crime was committed. Which it was. But I don't "know" that.

"I know. I know." He ran a hand through his short hair. "I'm just concerned about her." He paused. "Reese, I'm not asking you to tell me what all she said, or what she might've told medical, but . . . in your opinion, what happened between her and Stanton?"

I didn't look away but didn't answer, either.

He sighed. "I'm just trying to get a handle on the situation here. Give me something so I know what to do."

I opened my mouth to speak but hesitated before suggesting he put Kim on light duty. That usually meant working in dispatch, which was right down the hall from Stanton's office. While she had no business being out on patrol right now, especially in this heat, putting her in dispatch would be beyond the pale.

"Please." His voice was soft, almost pleading. "Just help me out here."

"I don't think she and Stanton should be working in the same building." I cleared my throat. "Maybe she should go out on patrol with me."

Alejandro tilted his head. "Why?"

"Because then she'll be away from him." I swallowed. "And we can work traffic duty in housing on Camp Shields. Something easy."

His eyes narrowed slightly. "You hate traffic detail."

"Of course I do. But I don't think—" I caught myself and chewed my lip.

"Nothing leaves this office, Reese. Just say it."

I gulped. "I don't think she should be standing as a gate sentry because of the heat, and I don't think she should be responding to domestics because of the risk."

"Because of the . . ." Alejandro studied me for a moment, then exhaled. "Fucking idiot. Damn it. I was really hoping I was wrong."

"Did you actually think you were?"

"No. But hope springs eternal." He scrubbed a hand over his face. "And Stanton? Jesus. I know she's young, but you'd think any woman who's serious about her career would know better than to fuck her superior."

Under normal circumstances, I'd have agreed with him, though I'd have pointed out the particular breed of female Sailor who calculatedly slept her way to commendations and promotions. Not to mention the girls who joined the Navy and happily took advantage of the massively disproportionate dick-to-chick ratio in every command. In fact, up until yesterday, I'd leaned toward putting Lockhoff in the latter category. Now . . .

"So what are you going to do?" I asked.

"Not much, at this point. She's . . ." He picked up a leave chit from his desk. "She's requested leave. Said she'll be off-island for a while."

My mouth went dry. "When?"

"Tomorrow. Her leave starts at the end of shift today." He sighed, gazing down at the chit in his hand. "Maybe some time away will be good for her. Give her a chance to get her head together."

"Yeah. Maybe."

Alejandro set the chit aside and touched my arm. "You okay?"

"I'm fine." I avoided his eyes. "I just don't like being involved in this kind of thing. It—" The unspoken words tasted acidic, and I had to keep what little I knew confidential for now anyway. "It just seems like something that should be between them."

He laughed bitterly. "Yeah, well. If this comes out, it's going to be between them, his wife, and the entire chain of command."

And, if the truth comes out, a couple of JAG lawyers and a judge.

"Well—" I moistened my lips. "—I guess we'll just hope she comes back from leave and makes a fresh start."

He nodded. "Let's hope so."

I couldn't get Lockhoff or her situation out of my mind. My guilty conscience gnawed its way deeper every time I replayed our conversation. She must've loathed me after that.

Damn it. I needed to make things right with her. And let her know she wasn't actually alone—something I would've killed for in the not-too-distant past.

Catching up to Lockhoff was a challenge. Today, she was on patrol at Camp Shields, which was about forty-five minutes away, clear over by Kadena Air Base. At least if she'd been standing watch somewhere or posted at one of the gates, I could've gone there to talk to her. Patrol duty made her a moving target.

Toward the end of shift, I came up with a bullshit excuse to go back to the precinct. At least Weiss was used to Alejandro calling me in, so he didn't bat an eye. Why would he question getting in early from our own patrol, since this meant he could chill in dispatch or hang out in the smoke pit before heading home?

We turned our guns into the armory, and Weiss wandered outside. As much as I needed a cigarette myself, I hung around and shot the shit with MA1 Harris and a couple of the civilian contractors, all the while keeping an eye on the front door.

Two by two, the other MAs came back and headed into the armory to turn in their weapons. With every pair that returned, I had a harder time sitting still. My stomach was twisted into knots, my head going a million miles an hour, and nothing was going to calm down until I had a chance to talk to—

The door opened again, and two backlit silhouettes came in from outside. I knew in an instant the second one was Lockhoff. She was shorter than her partner, with a distinctly feminine profile that even the uniform and police belt couldn't quite hide, and I just . . . knew it was her.

The door banged shut, cutting off the blinding afternoon sun, and when my eyes adjusted, I was right—there she was.

"Hey, MA3." I pushed myself off the edge of the desk where I'd been sitting.

She halted, eyeing me warily, but didn't speak. I gestured for her to follow me out into the hallway.

She planted her feet. "I need to download." She gestured at the pistol on her hip.

"Okay. Can you meet me in one of the conference rooms, then?"

A thin eyebrow rose, her lips tightening with suspicion. But she nodded. "I'll be there in a minute."

She followed her partner toward the armory, and I went to wait for her. One room was occupied by a class, so she'd have no trouble figuring out which one I was in. I just hoped she actually came.

I paced in front of the rows of folding chairs, trying to will my heart to slow down before I wound up in medical. I wondered if I had time for a cigarette. The armory was pretty slow this time of day, after all. The guys in there liked taking their sweet time as it was, and at the end of shift, they might have a dozen MAs lined up to download their weapons.

But if I went out for a smoke, Lockhoff would probably come in here, see that I wasn't around, and take off. And then I'd never get any damned sleep. The cigarette could wait. This could not.

Boots hitting linoleum stopped me in my tracks, and I turned around as Lockhoff appeared in the doorway. She hovered there, arms folded across her buttoned-up camouflage blouse, but she didn't come in.

"You, um, wanted to see me?"

"Yeah." I faced her fully, sliding my hands into my pockets to keep from looking confrontational or defensive. "Listen, I feel really bad about yesterday."

Her features hardened, but she didn't say anything.

"Do you have any plans?" I asked. "For after work?"

The eyebrow rose again. She shifted her weight, her boot squeaking. "Uh, no. Why?"

"Let me buy you dinner. Maybe over on Camp Shields? At the E-club?"

Lockhoff tilted her head, studying me for a long moment. "Um. Okay. I guess?"

"Okay." I exhaled. We hadn't had The Conversation yet, but at least she was willing to talk. It was a start. "I need to drop Weiss off at home. Then I'll meet you there?"

She didn't move. "MA2, this—"

"This is off the record," I said quietly. "Just call me Reese."

She swallowed. "Okay. Reese. What exactly is going on? I mean, okay, I get it. You're sorry." She hugged herself tighter. "Do we really need to drag this out and make a big thing out of it?"

"I . . ." I struggled to hold her gaze. "Yes. I owe you more than an apology."

Her forehead creased. "Why?"

My stomach roiled with shame, guilt, and too many years of biting my tongue. Finally, I took a deep breath. "Because we might have more in common than you think."

CHAPTER 5
KIM

I wasn't totally sure why I'd agreed to see MA2 Marion. Reese. She'd already apologized a few times, and while I was still pissed off that she'd doubted me, I was obviously more over it than she was. There was nothing about this that could be resolved over greasy hamburgers and mason jar sodas.

But that last comment she'd made had me curious. Insanely curious.

We had more in common than I thought? I doubted she was pregnant, not unless she was much closer to MA1 Gutiérrez than I'd guessed, which only left . . .

No way. No fucking way.

I couldn't imagine it happening to her. Replaying that night, putting her in my place, I couldn't see it. Couldn't see her standing for one second of Stanton's bullshit. Even when she was stressed or scared, even when instinct took over, MA2 Marion—*Reese*—didn't lie down and take anything. I still got goose bumps thinking about an incident during training a few months back. We were supposed to be hit with pepper spray, and then fight off the Red Man—a trainer in a heavily padded red suit—before completing the obstacle course, all in the name of learning to defend ourselves and subdue suspects while enduring that intense pain.

Reese hadn't fought off the Red Man and then continued through the course. She'd taken all two hundred fifty pounds of him to the ground and beaten the ever-loving fuck out of him until Gutiérrez and two other guys pulled her off. When her fight instinct kicked in, she just didn't stop.

Stanton wouldn't have succeeded with her. No way. I didn't want to think about what kind of guy could. What kind of guy *had*.

So maybe it was just curiosity that had me following the winding road through the sugar cane farms and villages from White Beach to Camp Shields. Whatever it was, I'd told her I'd be there, so I didn't turn back when the gate came into sight. I slowed down as I approached the guard shack, but the sentry—a civilian contractor named Atsushi—knew me, and waved me through.

Not far beyond the gate was the Enlisted Club. The parking lot was nearly empty, since the place wasn't all that popular during the week, but I immediately homed in on Reese's car. It was a piece-of-shit rust bucket just like everybody else's on this island, mine included, but I'd seen it around enough to know it was hers.

I parked a few spaces down and stepped out into the thick heat. Two feet away from the car, my head spun and my vision started to narrow. Damn it. I grabbed a lamppost and stood for a moment, breathing slowly and evenly. This had happened a few times when I'd first come to Okinawa, when I wasn't quite used to the heat, but lately . . . well, I supposed I expected it. Fuck this pregnancy crap. Maybe I should've swung by the barracks and changed out of my uniform. At least a pair of shorts and flip-flops would keep me cooler than boots and all this camouflage.

Eventually, the lightheadedness passed. When I was sure my legs were going to stay under me, I continued across the parking lot and into the E-club.

Reese had already snagged a table near the windows along the far wall, away from the scattered families and clusters of uniformed guys. She was in uniform, too—the blue camouflage stood out against the reddish walls and curtains.

I pulled out the chair opposite her. "Hey."

"Hey." She clung to a half-finished mason jar of water or Sprite or something. "Thanks for coming."

"Don't worry about it." I took a seat and faced her across the checkered tablecloth. "So, you wanted to talk."

She nodded and started to speak, but a waitress appeared beside us. I ordered an ice water, and when the woman had gone, faced Reese again. She took a deep breath. "Listen, I'll get right to the point. I haven't been able to stop thinking about yesterday because . . . God." She rubbed the back of her neck and then let her arm drop onto the table. "I promised myself a long time ago I'd never be the cop who questioned another woman's claim that she'd been assaulted. Ever. And then, yesterday, I did, and . . ." She exhaled hard. "I am so sorry, MA3."

"Kim."

Her eyebrows flicked up. "Hmm?"

"Kim." I swallowed. "My name's Kim."

"Oh. And you're, um, okay with me . . ."

"We're in uniform, but we're not at work."

"True. I guess we're not." She avoided my eyes. "I'm . . . The reason I wanted to see you tonight. I . . ."

Cautiously, I said, "We have something in common?"

"Yeah." She cleared her throat, and her hands suddenly seemed unsteady, shaking slightly as she wrung them behind the half-empty mason jar. "Which is why I felt especially bad about not taking you seriously right away. It's . . ." She squirmed, her lips pulling tight, and then she gave a humorless laugh. "I'd talked myself into explaining what happened to me, and now—"

"Don't." I leaned forward and lowered my voice. "I can read between the lines."

Her lips thinned as she searched my eyes.

"Don't," I repeated. "I know how hard it is to talk about it."

Reese exhaled. "Yeah. It is. So when you tried to talk to me about what happened, I acted like a bitch. And I'm sorry."

"I know you are. And it's water under the bridge."

"Are you sure?"

"Yeah. We're cool."

Right then, the waitress arrived at the table with my drink, and I took a long swallow to moisten my dry mouth. "Out of curiosity, would you have believed me if I didn't have the reputation I do?"

Reese blinked.

I waved a hand. "Yes, I know what people say about me."

Shaking her head, she sighed. "You're absolutely right. And I know I shouldn't have judged you like that."

I watched her for a moment. "Hypothetically, if I hadn't gotten out of the car yesterday, would you still have taken me to the SARC if I'd asked you to?"

"Of course!" She stared at me in horror. "I'd never keep you from filing a report."

"And if I'd wanted to make a statement to you, would you have taken it?"

"In a heartbeat."

I played with my straw and shrugged. "That's all I needed. You know how it is. You're a cop. You don't have to believe anyone. That's what judges and juries are for."

"Still, I—"

"Reese." I folded my arms on the table and leaned a little closer. "You're a good cop. The fact that you're trying to make this right says a lot."

She chewed her lip. "I just feel awful. I know I jumped to some really shitty conclusions, and . . . Hell, even if I was right about them, I had—"

"I might've done the same, to be honest."

Reese's lips parted. "What?"

"Look, I'm not stupid. I know how people see me, and I've thought the same about other girls. It's not really possible to be in the military without getting kind of cynical about everyone, you know?"

"I'll give you that."

"And, um . . ." I hesitated, then took a breath. "I actually knew a girl who filed a bullshit sexual assault report."

Reese groaned, rolling her eyes. "Please tell me that's not true."

"It is." I scowled. "This E4 at my first command was banging her way through the ranks while we were at sea. And that wasn't just rumors—we'd all caught her and her dick of the week hiding somewhere on the ship while we were making the rounds at night."

She laughed dryly. "People do get creative when they fuck on a boat, don't they?"

"Yeah, they do." I managed a slight laugh myself, but it didn't last. "Anyway, Senior Chief found out she'd slept with a married chief and decided to make an example out of both of them. Before that came out, though, she was *bragging* to a couple of girls in the berthing that she'd nailed Chief that night. The minute Senior Chief decided to charge them? She said Chief raped her." I gritted my teeth at the memory. "Why do you think it took me so long to even consider reporting Stan—reporting what happened?"

Reese squirmed uncomfortably, hugging herself as if she were cold in spite of her heavy uniform. "What . . . what happened to them?"

"Don't know. I gave my statement and transferred before they'd gotten very far into the investigation. I never heard how it turned out."

"They probably hemmed him up," she growled, rubbing a hand over her face. "And she probably stayed in and got promoted. But then when someone is *really* assaulted . . ."

"Right? And when it really happens, it's in a command like this where it'll blow up in the victim's face." I shook my head and went for my drink again. "So, I get it. I get why you questioned me. To be perfectly honest, I might've done the same thing. But I still would've taken a statement and taken the person to the SARC, and so would you. So . . ." I shrugged, then brought my glass up to take another swallow.

She folded her fingers under her chin. "I was definitely wrong about you."

"Oh yeah?"

Some color rushed into her cheeks, and she nodded. "I won't try to excuse it. I was wrong about you, and I'm sorry."

I set my glass down and folded my hands. "Then maybe we could start fresh."

She met my eyes. "Really?"

"Yeah. I mean, I don't know about you, but I could really use a female friend here."

"I understand that. We're a million miles from home, surrounded by guys. It does get a little . . . isolating after a while." She chewed her lip for a second. "Even without this shit going on, we could *all* use girlfriends."

"Exactly. So we start over, then? From the top?"

"Yeah. From the top." We both smiled, and for the first time in a long time, I felt some of the tension in my chest subside.

"And for the record," I said, "nothing you've heard about me is true. I have not slept with every—"

"You don't have to defend yourself to me, Kim." She reached across the table and gently placed her hand on my arm. "Your personal life is your business."

"I know." I swallowed. "But I need someone on this island to believe me."

"Okay. Tell me. Whatever it is."

I looked down at her hand on my wrist. "The way I dress and party, it's . . ." I shook my head. "It doesn't mean I sleep with every man who looks at me. I've never slept with a man on this island." I paused, stomach churning. "Except for . . ."

She squeezed my arm. "He doesn't count." Her lip curled slightly as she added, "I don't think he even counts as a man."

I actually laughed at that and patted her hand.

She smiled and sat back but quickly turned serious. "And yes, I do believe you."

"Thanks," I whispered.

"Look, I . . ." She took a deep breath and held my gaze. "I just, I want you to know, if you need anything, even if it's just someone to talk to . . . I'm here."

I smiled in spite of the lump rising in my throat. "Thank you." Then I lowered my gaze. "At least I probably won't be in this predicament"—I gestured at my stomach—"too much longer."

Her eyes widened. "What do you mean?"

"I'm, uh, taking leave." I drummed my fingers on the table. "I'm flying out tomorrow, and . . ." I couldn't bring myself to say it. I still hadn't quite accepted I was *doing* it.

"Do you need someone with you?" she asked quietly.

Yes. Yes, I so do.

But I shook my head. "No, I'll be okay."

"Are you sure?"

I nodded.

"Well, if you need anything, just text me. Here, let me give you my number."

We took out our phones and exchanged numbers as well as email addresses, and that tension in my chest eased a little more. Maybe we'd gotten off on the wrong foot, but I finally felt like I had an ally.

And with everything that lay ahead, I was going to need one.

CHAPTER 6
REESE

I didn't see Kim again before she left the island. According to Alejandro, she took an early-morning military flight from Kadena Air Base and was on her way to Hawaii, but she hadn't specified why she was going. Not to me anyway, and if Alejandro knew, he wasn't at liberty to disclose it.

I hoped to God she just needed to get away from Okinawa and planned to spend the time soaking up the sun on another set of white-sand beaches, since every beach on this island was too damned close to Stanton. Maybe she just needed a little space to collect her thoughts.

My gut feeling said otherwise, though. She hadn't spelled it out, but . . .

Twenty minutes before my shift started, I wandered into the precinct, desperate for coffee since the nicotine wasn't keeping me awake. Some of the guys were milling around the office, enjoying the air-conditioning while they could before going out on patrol.

And it didn't take but five minutes for them to start.

"Where's Lockhoff?" Barkley leaned on the front desk, coffee cup in hand. "She have to get some poor dude's dick surgically removed from her box?"

The guys chuckled. A sick feeling coiled in my stomach.

"Maybe she moved to night shift." MA3 Jensen snickered. "Fresh meat, right?"

More laughter. More of that awful, sick feeling.

"I think she went on leave," MA2 Lee said. "I saw a leave chit with her name on it. Didn't look at the dates, though."

Jensen shrugged. "Don't know. But, man, have you seen her recently?" He pointed over his shoulder toward the main office. "She had her blouse off yesterday, just her T-shirt on, and holy shit." He cupped his hands a few inches in front of his own chest. "She has got some serious titties going on."

"Let's hope she comes to the next barbecue, then." MA2 Lee whistled. "She wears one of those bikini tops again? Aww shit."

The other guys laughed.

"Yeah, she'll probably be out to here, though." Barkley made a gesture like he was conjuring a potbelly in front of himself. "Tits like that? I'll bet my next paycheck somebody done knocked that girl up."

I couldn't listen to it, so I topped off my coffee and started to get the hell out of there, but not before some more of the shit-talking made it to me:

"Man, I would tap that. And hey, long as she's got the kid in there—bareback all the way!"

"No way, dude. Girl like her? I wouldn't go in without a raincoat on."

"I wouldn't go in without a hazmat suit on."

"Definitely wouldn't put my face down—"

"*Hey.*" I spun around in the doorway and glared at them. "Is this really how you're going to talk about a fellow cop?"

Jensen put up his hands. "Whoa. Sorry, MA2. But seriously, you've seen—"

"Let's get back out on patrol." Lee smacked Barkley's arm. "We might get to Camp Shields in time to see the moms doing their yoga in the park."

"Fuckers." I stormed out of the office to the smoke pit, which was, thank God, empty. My hands were shaking so badly, I could barely get a cigarette out of the pack, never mind light it, but I finally succeeded and pulled in some smoke.

I needed to quit smoking, but I didn't see that happening anytime soon. Not until I got out of the Navy or transferred to a better command, anyway. My last deployment had driven me to start smoking. Alejandro had transferred back from Gitmo with a snuff habit, and I'd given him all kinds of shit for that—wasn't like he didn't know how poisonous it was—until I'd come home from Afghanistan smoking a pack and a half a day. Now I was pushing two and a half. Much longer on this island and I'd be a goddamned chain smoker.

As I took another drag, a lead ball of guilt formed in my stomach. A week ago, I'd have been part of that conversation in the office. I probably would've come up with even cruder comments than they had. If I'd learned anything since I'd enlisted, it was that fitting in with these guys was the safest approach. If they're being crass, be crasser. If they're drunk, get drunker. If they think a girl's a slut, declare her a whore with a pussy like a wizard's sleeve.

But that didn't excuse the things I'd said. And I didn't let myself wonder how many other women I'd misjudged because that train of thought would have taken me right through this pack of smokes.

Weiss stepped out of the precinct. "Hey, MA2. We heading out on patrol?"

"Yeah." I snuffed out my dying cigarette. "Just need to arm up."

"All right." He walked past me as I came down from the smoke pit. "You do that, and I'll have a smoke."

"Okay. Back in a minute."

On my way to the armory, I passed Stanton's office, and the sound of his voice through the closed door gave me chills.

"Well, I dodged a bullet with that one, that's for sure." He chuckled, and I stopped dead in my tracks. "She had me worried."

Someone laughed, and it took me a second to recognize Chief Wolcott's voice. "Yeah, if you'd had to explain this to Susan, you could've sold tickets to the fireworks show."

A third person laughed, and my heart sank.

Alejandro? You? Please, no . . .

"You're a braver man than I am, Sir." That was definitely his voice.

"What can I say?" Stanton said. "Have you seen the ass on that girl?"

"Yeah, can't blame you." Chief's low voice was obviously not meant to carry out of the room. "That girl offered it up, I might take a shot at it myself."

"Yeah, right." Alejandro snickered. "Talk all the shit you want, Chief." It sounded like he'd clapped the man's arm. "We all know you're afraid of Tomi."

"Lieutenant's afraid of *his* wife and that didn't stop him!"

"Well," Stanton said, "what she doesn't know won't hurt me, will it?"

All three of them laughed. I didn't know if I wanted to knock the door down and kick their asses, or lean against the wall and cry.

Chief Wolcott. Alejandro. Two members of our chain of command—two people who could've been allies for Lockhoff—laughing and joking with the man who'd assaulted her. I knew how this would end: if she reported what happened to either of them now, they'd brush it off because they already believed Lieutenant Stanton.

It was just as well Lockhoff was off-island at the moment.

Because back here on Okinawa, she had nowhere to go.

CHAPTER 7
KIM

Well, that step was done.

I walked out of the clinic, paperwork in hand, and took a deep breath of the humid Hawaiian air. I'd made the appointment. Off-base, of course—it wouldn't have cost me anything to have it done at the hospital on Tripler Air Base just down the road, but there was no way I wanted this in my military medical record. I couldn't risk anyone asking questions that might raise *more* questions.

Now everything was scheduled. In T minus three days, this would be over. Nothing could change what had happened, but I wouldn't be pregnant with Stanton's baby anymore.

Only one problem: someone had to drive me to and from the clinic and stay with me for forty-eight hours in case of . . . complications.

I shuddered at the thought and tried not to remember all the things the nurse had mentioned as potential problems. Everything had to go smoothly. It just had to. I could barely cope as it was. And God help me if I had to take more leave to recover. That would require explanations I wasn't ready to give, money I couldn't afford to pay.

The papers in my hand seemed to weigh a hundred pounds, and I felt like I was knee-deep in wet cement as I walked back to my rental car.

I dropped into the driver's seat and started the engine. For a moment, I just closed my eyes and let the air-conditioning blow in my face. I wasn't particularly hot, but the cool air felt nice, and I was all about clinging to anything that didn't feel *bad*.

Eventually, though, I shook myself awake. I needed to get the fuck away from this place. At least until I had to come back at 0700 sharp on Friday morning.

I drove to the shithole motel near Tripler on autopilot. I keyed myself into the cold, empty room—the AC was constantly in high gear—shut the door, and leaned against it.

What the hell was I supposed to do now?

I looked around the room, as if it could offer some answers. The envelope full of cash was still sitting beneath the television. I'd left it there by mistake, but after I'd realized where it was, I'd secretly hoped the maids would steal it.

I'm sorry, I could hear myself telling Stanton over the phone. *The money's gone. I can't get it done.*

But no. All the money was there. Down to the last hundred-dollar bill.

And even if it had been gone, he'd have just sent me more. Or ordered me to bite the bullet and go to military medical.

Damn. I should've just had it done on Okinawa. But then there'd be no hiding it. And I didn't even know if abortions were legal on Okinawa, let alone if I'd be able to find an English-speaking doctor.

The doctor at the clinic here on Oahu had spoken perfect English, of course. The nurse who'd seen me had, anyway. She'd understood every word I said, and she'd understood that I was scared.

This isn't an easy thing, she'd told me gently. *We're going to take good care of you, but it's okay to be nervous.*

How the hell was I supposed to explain I wasn't scared of the procedure? Well, okay, I *was* scared of it, but I was fucking terrified of what would happen if I *didn't* get it done.

My stomach turned, and I swallowed hard to keep what little I'd eaten where it belonged. I pushed myself off the door, took a few steps, and sank onto the foot of the rock-hard, neatly made bed. Breathing slowly, I cradled my head in my hands.

This wasn't how things were supposed to work out. Being "that girl"—the Sailor who got herself knocked up and had an abortion before the rumors got out of hand—was never part of my plans, especially since I didn't do the necessary things to get myself knocked up. I'd had my heart set on a military career since I was a teenager. Everything had been laid out, planned from here to retirement. Forget twenty years. This Sailor was staying in for thirty, retiring as a master chief. I refused to consider anything less.

Single motherhood wasn't something I could cope with. I'd already watched my own mother struggle to raise me alone, and there was no way in hell I was putting myself through that. I had a career plan, damn it, and I was well on my way to making it happen.

Though, so far, it was hell.

I loved the job itself. I loved seeing the world, working on ships and bases and steadily moving up the ranks. With my most recent eval, I was pretty much a shoo-in to make MA2.

When I'd enlisted, I'd had no idea what I was getting myself into. From the beginning—all through boot camp, school, a deployment, shore duty—I'd felt more alone than I ever had in my life. My last command thought I was a bitch and a cold fish. This command thought I was a ditzy whore, and thanks to Okinawa being so isolated, I didn't have anyone *except* my command.

And what good did they do me now, while I sat alone in Hawaii, facing down a procedure that scared the hell out of me?

I'd never even considered how I felt about abortion. I was a lesbian. Accidental pregnancies were as much a part of my reality as athletic cups and prostate exams.

God, this was a nightmare. I didn't know how to feel. What to think. Which way was up. Was this the right thing to do? The wrong one? I couldn't even fit *I'm pregnant* into my head. How was I supposed to make a decision about something I couldn't begin to comprehend?

I ran my fingers through my hair and choked back my tears. No crying. I'd done enough of that. Hormones and stress had already gotten the best of me twice today. No more crying, damn it. It wouldn't solve anything.

Solve anything?

I laughed bitterly and lay back on the bed, staring up at the water-stained ceiling. There was no solving this. No matter what happened at that clinic on Friday morning, this situation still existed. I'd still been raped by a man with too much power and influence to be afraid of repercussions. I still had to answer to that man.

And here in Hawaii, still confused and still pregnant, I was still alone.

I got up and grabbed my laptop off the table beside the bed. The motel's Wi-Fi wasn't great, but it connected, and before I could question what I was doing, I opened up my email and sent a message to Reese's work address.

Need to talk to someone ASAP—do you have Skype?
And I waited.

CHAPTER 8
REESE

The instant I saw the message from Kim, my heart went into my throat. The millions of worst-case scenarios that had kept me up all last night went through my head. I quickly replied, and we exchanged Skype handles. As soon as my laptop had connected, I pinged her, and thank God, she was online.

As soon as Kim appeared on the screen, my gut twisted. She was pale, and eye makeup had left muddy streaks down both sides of her face.

"Hey," I said, trying to keep the worry out of my voice and expression. "Where are you?"

"I'm in Hawaii." She wiped her eyes. "To get . . . to get an abortion."

My heart dropped. "How are you holding up?"

"I'm not. I'm kind of freaking out."

"About the . . ." I hesitated. "About—"

"The abortion." She shuddered. "And they told me today, I have to have someone with me." She kept her gaze down. "To drive me to and from and to stay with me. While I . . ." Kim swallowed, and maybe it was just the webcam, but it looked like she lost some color. "While I recover."

"When is it scheduled?"

She winced. "Friday morning. 0700. I'm scared to death, and I don't know where the hell I'm going to find someone here who—"

"I'll be there."

Kim blinked. "You . . . really?"

"I'll . . ." Shit. Logistics. "I'll find a way. You shouldn't be there alone."

"But . . ."

"Do you need someone there with you?"

She bit her lip, then nodded slowly, and God, she looked like a scared little girl. I wanted so bad to go through the computer and hug her. No two ways about it: I was going to Hawaii if I had to threaten Alejandro over my leave chit.

"I'll get Gutiérrez to sign off on a leave chit, and I'll work out a flight. Can you hang in there until then?"

Kim nodded. She smiled, and though she was still obviously tense, it seemed genuine. "Thank you."

"You're welcome. I'll be there as soon as I can."

Less than an hour after I chatted with Kim, I handed the emergency leave chit to Alejandro.

"What's this?"

"MA3 Lockhoff is in Hawaii and . . ." I swallowed, not sure how much to divulge. "I don't think she should be alone right now."

He eyed the chit, then looked at me. "Does that qualify as an emergency?"

"Ask Stanton. I'm sure he'll sign off on it."

His eyebrows rose. "Is there something I should know about?"

"Please. Just sign the chit."

He glanced down at the paper. "Wait here."

"What?"

"Just wait here." He gestured at one of the chairs in front of his desk. "I'll be back in a minute." He didn't wait for a response before he headed out of the office.

I texted Weiss: *Stuck in MA1's office for a few.*

Not ten minutes after Alejandro had gone, I heard him coming down the hall.

"Hey, Weiss," he called out. "You're in dispatch."

I cringed. I owed Weiss a drink for that. Poor dude always got stuck in dispatch when I had to step away from patrol. Which meant . . .

Oh, please, Alejandro. Tell me it's approved.

He stepped into the office and handed me the chit. "Go pack and get some sleep. Your leave starts now and there's a Space-A flight tomorrow morning. Be at the terminal at 0200. I'll make sure you're a priority one."

I nodded. "Thank you."

He held my gaze. "I appreciate you doing this for her."

I hesitated. "Well, someone has to help sweep things under the rug, right?"

"Better you than me." Alejandro chuckled, and the sick feeling in my stomach intensified. He really was on Stanton's side, wasn't he? That would explain why he'd hand-routed the chit and gotten all the signatures in record time—he knew damn well Stanton didn't want anything interfering with what Kim was doing.

No wonder Kim had caved in and gone to Hawaii.

She really *didn't* have any allies.

Space Available flights were always a gamble, and it looked like I was up against a lot of people this morning. At least a hundred sleepy-eyed service members and dependents were crammed into the terminal area, nervously watching the screens and counting down the minutes until roll call. I had to get on this flight. Had to. If I didn't, the next one wasn't until Friday morning, which would be too late.

While I waited, I ran through some contingency plans in my head. There was no way in hell I could afford a commercial ticket, especially not on such short notice. If I couldn't be there to help Kim, maybe I could get someone else to help out. It wouldn't be ideal, having a complete stranger taking care of her during that kind of emotional havoc, but in the absence of other options . . .

On my phone, I scrolled through my Facebook friends to see if any of them were still stationed at Tripler or Pearl Harbor. I didn't dare send a male. Though they were decent guys, the last thing Kim needed right now was to be drugged out of her mind, in terrible pain, *and* at the mercy of a man she didn't know.

Fortunately, it turned out there was a Patriot Express flight leaving today—a passenger jet that went to Seattle via Iwo Kuni and Yokota—and most of the people crowded in here were getting on that flight, not the one to Hawaii. After roll call for Seattle, only five of us remained.

I exhaled. The plane to Hawaii had twenty-three seats available.

The flight was on time, thank God, and they didn't even bother doing a formal roll call since there were so few of us. With every step of the process—check-in, security, transport to the plane—I was sure someone was going to come out and tell us the flight was canceled at the last second. It had happened to me before.

But then I was on the chilly cargo jet. The engines were started, and the crew was getting situated. We were really leaving.

Before they told us to stow our electronics, I sent a quick email to Kim:

Onboard. I'll be there in a few hours. Hang in there.

Once I'd gotten off the plane and made it through customs, I hurried to baggage claim where she'd said she'd meet me.

I scanned the thin crowd. On the third glance, I realized she was right there, but I barely recognized her at all. Though I'd seen her in civvies before, she looked like another woman entirely, and I couldn't put my finger on why. It wasn't even the early signs of pregnancy—though the top of her T-shirt fit differently now, she wasn't showing yet.

Her smile was weak but may as well have been a huge beaming grin for all it lit up the terminal.

I stepped out of the secure zone and was so damned relieved to see her, I gave her a hug.

She stiffened at first, and I thought for a second that I'd overstepped my bounds, but then she wrapped her arms around me and relaxed.

She barely whispered, "Thank you so much for coming, MA2."

"You can still call me Reese." I stroked her hair and added, "No ranks. We're not at work."

"Okay."

"How are you holding up?"

As she let me go, she shrugged. "Holding up."

Well, it was something.

We loaded my seabag into the trunk of her rental car and left the base. While she drove and we made small talk, I surreptitiously watched her, trying to figure out what had changed.

She normally wore makeup that *just* toed the lines of what the Navy would allow. In civvies, she went all out, even for casual functions like command barbecues and softball games. Today, she had on a little bit of mascara, and she might have had something on her lips, but it was so subtle, I couldn't tell.

The plain T-shirt was loose and comfortable, the shorts short enough to keep her cool in this heat but still long enough to cover up the butterfly tattoo that was usually *quite* visible in civvies, despite being halfway up her inner thigh. Instead of strappy sandals, she had on a simple pair of flip-flops.

Though she looked exhausted, especially with no makeup to hide the dark circles under her eyes, she was . . . Wow. Even when I hadn't had a high opinion of her, she'd caught my eye, but like *this*, she messed with my pulse. I was a sucker for the natural look, and even when stress and exhaustion had taken their toll, Kim was one of those women who didn't need much, if any, makeup. She also didn't need the push-up bras and stripper heels she was so fond of. It was a crime that someone like her thought she needed any enhancement when she looked this good in her own skin.

At a stoplight, she glanced at me. "You want to grab lunch?"

"I could go for some coffee if nothing else."

"Yeah, me too."

We found a fast-food dive a couple of blocks from the air base gates and grabbed a corner table below the air conditioner.

Kim wrapped both hands around a water bottle. "I feel a lot better now that you're here."

"Good." I watched her for a moment. "How are you doing, though? With everything?"

"I'm . . ." She picked at the label on the bottle. Then her shoulders dropped, and though she kept herself together, it was like a dam had broken inside her. "I'm a mess, Reese."

I took her hand and squeezed it. "I know you are. I wish there was more I could do."

"There, um . . ." Kim closed her eyes and took a breath before meeting my gaze. "There is, actually."

"There is? What?"

"Look, I know you're a mandated reporter. But . . . I need to tell someone." Her eyebrows pulled together. "I'm not going to file anything, but I need someone to know what happened. Especially before tomorrow."

I fidgeted. This was dangerous ground. "I *can't* keep it quiet, though. There are civilian advocates you can talk to."

She reached across the table and put her hand on my arm. "Reese, you're the only one from the island I can trust. Everyone else is in Stanton's back pocket."

"What about here? There has to be someone at Pearl or even Tripler who—"

"No." Kim shook her head. "He's been in way too long. Knows way too many people. I can't trust anyone else except for you, and I . . ." Her eyes welled up, and she swiped at them. "I can't keep carrying this by myself."

My chest ached. I gnawed my lip. White Beach was a tiny, isolated base on a tiny, isolated island. Most of the commands tended to stick together—aviators hung out with aviators, cops hung out with cops. Which meant when bad things happened, the only person a cop could lean on was . . . another cop. Who would be required by the UCMJ to report something like this or risk being charged with dereliction of duty.

I took her hand and squeezed it gently. "Kim, you know what happened, not me. But whatever did happen, if you need help, you've got to talk to someone."

"Who?" She met my eyes, and hers were wide with desperation. "Gutiérrez is buddy-buddy with Stanton. All the chiefs have their noses wedged between Stanton's ass cheeks. He's got friends all the way up to the captain." She sniffed sharply. "There's literally no one I can talk to who isn't either Stanton's golfing buddy or another cop. And anyone here?" Kim scowled and shook her head. "God knows who *they* know."

"What about the SARC?" Even as I said it, my heart sank a little. That asshole came by the precinct quite often, ostensibly to be present and visible, as well as to discuss solutions with the higher-ups. That illusion might've stuck if we hadn't all heard some of his and Stanton's conversations through the office door. I was no expert, but I was pretty sure sexual assault prevention didn't involve birdies and nine irons. And if our SARC was fucked up, there was no way to be sure the ones on this island wouldn't be, too. Especially now that several people in sexual assault response departments throughout the military had been strung up recently for sexual assault themselves.

Fact was, there was no one I could suggest to her because I wouldn't have trusted any of them with my own report.

"Or maybe not the SARC." I shook my head. "God, I'm so sorry."

"Damn it." She rubbed her temples. "This is so messed up."

"I know. I'm sorry."

"It's not your fault. You're trying to be a good cop."

"I want to be a good friend, too."

She met my gaze, eyebrows climbing her forehead.

"I do," I whispered. "I'm guilty of judging you before, and I can't apologize enough for that. But . . . Look, I'm not just here to help a junior Sailor."

A faint smile pulled at her lips. "Thank you."

I returned the smile, but hers and mine both faded quickly. I folded my hands on the table. "I want to help you, Kim. I do."

"I know."

"And I'm happy to come with you tomorrow, but I need you to tell me: is that really what you want to do?"

"It's . . ."

My heart clenched. "It's okay. You can tell me."

She shifted her gaze away. "I, um . . . Look, without going into any detail that you'd have to repeat, he's got me in a bad spot."

I blinked. "How so?"

"He said if I had the baby, he'd use his parental rights." She played with the hem of her shirt. "Prevent me from putting it up for adoption, demand visitation, all of that."

"Oh Jesus." I ground my teeth. "Is that son of a bitch unaware that you could get a protective order against him?"

She met my eyes. "And what happens with that when he's found not guilty by a jury of *his* peers?"

I winced. Damn it.

She stiffened. "Fuck . . ."

"It's okay." I put my hand on her forearm. "This is still between us." Oh, but we were walking a dangerously thin line.

"Thanks." She set her shoulders back and held my gaze. "Anyway, when I go back to Okinawa, he won't have that card to play anymore."

"That's . . . I guess that's true." How morbid. An abortion as an ace up her sleeve? He really had backed her into a fucked-up corner, hadn't he?

Kim studied me. "How about this? I'll tell you everything. A week after we get back to Okinawa, if I haven't reported it, then . . . do what you have to do."

I wrung my hands under the table. It sounded reasonable on the surface but still left a lot of time for this to blow up in our faces. And yet, how willingly would I have severed an arm just to have someone listen to me back when I'd been in an all-too-similar position?

"Okay," I said. "One week from the time we get back to Okinawa."

She nodded. "Okay. One week." She closed her eyes and took a deep breath. "For starters, like I've mentioned, I know everyone in our command thinks I'm a slut." She wiped her eyes. "But I'm not."

I gnawed my lower lip. A short time with Kim and my attitude about her had certainly been adjusted. "I know you're not."

She went on. "The thing is, I was a completely different person at my last command."

I rested my forearms on the edge of the table. "How so?"

"I was . . . I didn't party with the guys, that's for sure. I pretty much kept my head down. When a guy came on to me, I tried to be polite about not being interested, but somehow that got turned into me being a cold fish."

I exhaled. "Yeah, I can relate."

"Really?"

I nodded. "I get that at this command. All the time."

"Fun, isn't it?"

"Seriously."

Kim plucked a napkin from the dispenser on the table and started tearing off little pieces. "They all talked about what an ice queen I was. How security at Fort Knox had nothing on my pussy." Her cheeks reddened, and she stared at her hands as she continued shredding napkin. "They nicknamed me Razor Wire."

"Razor Wire?"

She nodded. "One of the guys spent half the Navy Ball hitting on me. When I turned him down for the hundredth time that night, he went and told the others he couldn't get through the razor wire in Lockhoff's pants." She laughed bitterly. "And the name stuck."

My heart dropped into the pit of my stomach. "Oh my God. That's horrible."

"It's not the worst of it." She set the tattered napkin down and hugged herself, still avoiding my eyes. "A few times, I overheard guys in my command saying I just needed a dick to pound some sense into me so I'd stop being such a bitch."

My blood turned cold. Wasn't *that* a familiar sentiment . . .

She ran an unsteady hand through her hair. "I was scared. I thought, you know, they might do something to 'reform' Razor Wire. So when I came to Okinawa, I did what all the popular girls at my last command did." She sighed. "Aside from actually sleeping with any of them, anyway. But I drank with them, partied with them, acted like the slutty little thing they all wanted. And what a surprise, that backfired, too."

"How so?"

She met my eyes.

I took a deep breath. "So what happened with Stanton?"

Lowering her gaze, Kim shivered. "We were at a retirement party. Senior Chief O'Leary, a few months ago."

"Right."

"I'd had a few beers, but I was still pretty steady on my feet." She drummed her fingernails on the table. "And then Stanton comes up and starts talking to me. And, I mean, he's a lieutenant. He's the fucking security officer. I'm just a third class, and . . . I guess I was kind of blown away that he was even talking to me. Officers don't usually give us the time of day, you know?" She reached up and rubbed the bridge of her nose. "I thought it was a nice switch to talk to someone who could string a sentence together without *fuck* being every other word."

I nodded. Though I didn't say it out loud—no sense adding insult to injury—the fact was, Stanton could be charming when he wanted to be. He was made of slime and bullshit, but once in a while . . .

I cleared my throat to mask a shudder. "What happened after that?"

"He offered me a lift home, and . . ." She covered her face with her hands for a second. "God, I feel so stupid. I just thought he was being nice." Swearing under her breath, she dropped her hands. "One minute he was driving me home. Then he pulls into this parking lot over by Tengan Pier. You know, way out in the middle of nowhere."

I nodded, a sick feeling coiling in my gut. The first time I'd had to guard the long, mostly empty pier, Alejandro had joked that, *At Tengan Pier, no one can hear you scream.* Suddenly that comment wasn't so funny.

I sipped my coffee. "Yeah, I know the place."

"I should've known something was up. I don't even know what I was thinking at that point, and then he kissed me, and I was so . . ." Her eyes unfocused, and she slowly shook her head. "I was so caught off guard at first, I didn't do anything. But then I tried to push him away. That was when he reached across and hit the lever for the seat back. It reclined. He pushed me onto my back and started pushing my skirt up." Kim hugged herself tighter and shivered. "I told him to stop, but he ignored me. I tried to put my legs together, but he kept his knee between them."

"Jesus," I breathed. I hoped to God if she saw the sweat beading along my hairline, she'd write it off as the heat and humidity, and that she didn't notice the way I was gripping the side of my chair with one hand.

"He was on top, and . . . when he unzipped his shorts, I panicked. I told him over and over that I didn't want to do this, and I told him to stop, and he just . . ." She was silent for a moment, still staring at the table, unfocused. Her whole body trembled, and the fluorescent lights overhead picked out the way she was starting to sweat just like I was.

"We can take a break if you need to." My cop voice sounded weird to my own ears, but shifting into that mode, being a cop instead of a woman who'd been there, meant I stood a chance of getting through this conversation. "Take your time."

She went quiet again, but only for a minute or so. "I just felt like . . ." She swiped at her eyes with a trembling hand. "Look at me. I'm a foot shorter than him. I can hold my own at PT, but that guy . . . he's *built*."

"Yeah, he is."

"And there was something about the way he was looking at me, and holding me down, that told me there was no point in fighting." She gnawed her lower lip. "Like, this was happening whether I liked it or not, and the only say I had in the matter was whether I was bruised and bloody afterward. I could fight him or I could let him, but he was going to. So I . . ." She buried her face in her hands for a moment, then dropped them to her lap and lifted her gaze, her eyes wet. "I let him. I never said yes. I never told him I wanted it. I just stopped fighting, and I . . ." She sniffed sharply as a tear slid down her cheek. "I let him."

"But you told him no, didn't you?"

"Yes, but—"

"Then he didn't—"

"I know." She wiped her eyes. "But you try convincing all the guys who think I'm a whore and all of Stanton's best buddies that I didn't want it. When you're a girl like me, anything short of clawing at his face and screaming, 'No!' is as good as 'yes.' You and I both know it's not, but our opinion and a judge's . . ."

The words hit me hard in the gut. I wanted so bad to tell her she was wrong. But I knew how fucked up our command was. I knew how badly the deck was stacked against her.

"I'm so sorry," I said, and that had never sounded so damned useless.

"I tried to be what I thought they wanted girls in the Navy to be, and . . ." She wiped her eyes. "It's like, now that they think I'm a slut, they're offended as hell if I reject them. All the guys at my last command thought I was a bitch for shutting them all out. All the guys here think I'm a bitch because they think I'm sleeping with everyone *but* them." She threw up her hands. "I don't know what to do."

"I know the feeling."

"You do?"

I nodded. "It starts in boot camp, and I don't think it ever fucking ends."

She groaned and buried her face in her hands again. "God . . ."

"I know. Believe me, I know."

"How do you deal with it?"

I shrugged. "I tried being whatever the guys were 'satisfied' with me being, but even that didn't work. Being myself doesn't work, either, so really, your guess is as good as mine."

Kim shuddered. "To be honest, being myself scares me more than anything else."

"Why's that?"

"Because I don't want—" Flinching, she cut herself off.

I leaned closer. "You don't want . . .?"

"My friend's sister is in the Army," Lockhoff said, barely whispering. "And she told me about how when the guys in her command found out she was a lesbian, they saw her as a challenge." She met my eyes. "I've already been threatened with corrective rape—more than once. I'm not painting a bull's-eye on my forehead."

I blinked. "Are you . . . are you telling me you're a lesbian?"

She broke eye contact. After a moment, she nodded.

I reached across the table and touched her arm. "It's okay. I won't tell."

With a humorless laugh, she said, "But you'll ask?"

"In confidence, yeah, I guess I will." I patted her arm before withdrawing my hand. "But you're not the only one, just so you know."

Her eyebrows jumped. "Are you . . .?"

I nodded, and something in my chest relaxed. I'd been dying to tell *someone* for a long time, and it was a relief even in this context. DADT was a distant memory, but coming out was still fucking terrifying.

Kim regarded me silently for a moment. "You're serious? You're a lesbian?"

"All the rumors didn't give it away?"

She waved a hand. "I don't take much seriously from the guys who also brag about getting me into bed."

I grimaced. "You've heard those, then?"

"Oh yeah."

"Ouch."

She shrugged. "I set myself up for it. Funny thing was, I acted like a whore because I thought it might make the rest of the command accept me. I didn't realize it would piss them all off." She scrubbed a hand over her face and cursed softly. "Who knew I was setting myself up for—"

"You didn't." I squeezed her other hand. "Don't you dare blame yourself."

She held my gaze and then released a breath. "You think it wouldn't have happened if I hadn't—"

"It doesn't make it right, Kim. You were playing the game as best you could. The blame for what happened is on Stanton. Not you."

Kim slouched in her chair. "I just hate the fact that no matter how much we both know that, it's not going to change anything. I'm the one who can't sleep at night and has to get an . . ." She swallowed hard. "And nothing is ever going to happen to him." As she ran her hand through her hair, her shoulders sagged even more and her gaze dropped.

My heart ached. God, I could see so much of myself in her. I had no idea what to do or say, but damn if I didn't know how it felt to hurt like that.

"Come here." I stood, and when she did the same, I wrapped my arms around her. "I'm so sorry all this has happened to you."

"Thank you."

"You're welcome." I hugged her tighter. "And I am *so* sorry for questioning you when—"

"Don't." She pulled back and looked up at me. "I promise, I'm not mad. I get it."

"But I—"

"Please," she whispered. "Don't. It's okay."

I exhaled. "Okay. When we get back and you go to report this, if you need someone to go to the SARC with you, just say the word."

"I will."

I released her and met her eyes. "For now, we *are* in Hawaii." I smiled cautiously. "Why don't we go to the motel, let me grab a shower, and then go out and blow off some steam?"

I'll be damned if she didn't finally smile back. "That sounds like a great idea."

CHAPTER 9
KIM

From the moment the second blue line had appeared on the home pregnancy test, I'd been a hot mess. Even worse than I'd been just after O'Leary's retirement party. Thoughts like having fun and going out just for the hell of it had become foreign concepts.

As Reese got dressed after grabbing a quick shower, I didn't even know where to go for the afternoon. I didn't know where to start. I'd been locked inside my head for so long, obsessing over things beyond my control, I had no idea what to do with myself now that I'd decided to take a breather.

I handed Reese the keys, and we climbed into the rental car. As she ran the AC to blow away the afternoon's heat, she glanced around. "Man, there isn't much in this area, is there?"

"No, it's kind of a shitty part of town. Was all I could afford."

"On this island? I don't doubt that. Honolulu would've set you back an entire paycheck."

"Right? I've gotten spoiled. Okinawa's cheap."

"That's for sure. Oahu's a fucking rip-off." She tapped her thumbs on the wheel for a moment. "Why don't we grab a bite to eat? You're going to be holed up in that place for a couple of days, so I'm thinking we should get some fresh air and decent food while we still can."

I wasn't sure if anything I ate would stay where it belonged, but I was willing to give it a try.

"Anything in particular you're in the mood for?" She turned to me. "I don't want to upset your stomach."

"My stomach's fine." *So far.*

"Is it? I thought . . . uh . . ."

"Thought I'm at that stage where I'm throwing up at the drop of a hat?"

"Basically, yeah."

"No, I'm good." I shook my head. "The fucked-up thing is I haven't even *had* any real morning sickness. The only time I've gotten sick has been when Stanton's nearby."

"Oh, honey." Reese waved a hand. "I'm not carrying his kid and *I* want to blow chunks whenever he shows up."

I wrinkled my nose. "He kind of has that effect, doesn't he?"

"There's no 'kind of' about it. He's a fucking creeper."

"He so is. But, yeah, for food? Anything. In fact, I'm a lot hungrier than I thought."

"Me too. Those little box meals they serve on the plane are a joke."

I laughed. "I don't know. They're better than commercial-airline food."

"Okay, I'll give you that. But stale room-temperature McDonald's is better than commercial-airline food."

"Good point."

We glanced at each other and both laughed.

She shifted the idling car into reverse and eased out of the parking space. "Why don't we head down to Waikiki? There's got to be some decent food down there."

"I'm in."

Getting out of that shithole, escaping reality to enjoy a meal with someone who wasn't judging or threatening me?

Yeah. I was in.

In Waikiki, Reese parked outside one of those shopping centers that catered to tourists with no taste and too much money. After wandering for a while through throngs of people in oversized sunglasses and bright Hawaiian shirts, we found a café overlooking a beautiful white-sand beach.

The hostess showed us to a table on the patio and gave us a couple of colorful, laminated menus.

For a few minutes, I just sat back and let the tropical wind play with my hair and warm my face. The climate here was almost identical to Okinawa, but at least for this afternoon, it didn't take me back to the island where *he* was waiting for me. If only for today, it was a reprieve from the freezing-cold motel room where I'd been on the verge of a breakdown.

I shifted my gaze toward Reese, watching her over the menu as she looked out at the ocean. I still couldn't believe she'd come. I'd begged her to get on Skype because I'd needed someone to listen to me and just be there so I didn't feel quite so alone. The last thing I'd expected was this. No questions asked, on a moment's notice, the woman who hadn't even liked me a week ago had taken leave, hopped a plane, and now . . . she was here.

Because we might have more in common than you think.

She hadn't said *exactly* what had happened, but I could connect the dots she'd given me. And there was no way I could be thankful it had happened to her just so we could find some common ground. I wouldn't have wished that on anyone.

But if there was even the slightest silver lining to any of this, then I was grateful.

She turned her head, and I almost dropped my menu. She raised her eyebrows. "You okay?"

"Yeah. Yeah, I . . ." *Was staring at you because—* "I'm good. Just zoned out a bit."

She smiled faintly. "I can't blame you. And if I nod off here at the table, don't take it personally."

I laughed. "Does that mean I have to drive back?"

"We'll see. But once I get a Red Bull or two in me, I'll be fine. I'm just a bit jet-lagged."

"Did you at least get some sleep on the plane?"

Reese nodded. "God, I love cargo jets. Nothing like being able to stretch out across the seats."

"Right? And the noise from the engines drowns out everything else. If it wasn't so damned cold, it would be *perfect*."

She shrugged. "I packed a blanket. I was good."

"Smart."

"You didn't?"

"No, no, I did. But there was a family on my flight who'd obviously never flown cargo class before."

"Ouch."

"Yeah."

Our eyes met, and I was sure an awkward *What the hell do we say now?* silence was about to set in, but the waitress picked that exact moment to materialize beside us.

"Have you had a chance to decide?" she asked.

"Um . . ." I glanced at the menu and realized I'd been so wrapped up in Reese, not a single item had registered. "Go ahead. I just need a second."

While Reese ordered, I quickly scanned the menu. Damn, all the fancy tropical drinks sounded ridiculously tempting. Getting drunk and stupid sounded even better.

But I settled on a virgin mai tai. After the waitress had gone away to get our orders, I shook my head. "I don't know why I didn't just order a real one. Seems kind of stupid, doesn't it? Worrying about alcohol when I'm . . ." I couldn't even finish the thought.

"No, it doesn't."

I swallowed. "But the only reason I wouldn't is because I'm pregnant. And after tomorrow . . ."

She winced and pursed her lips.

I played with the edge of the tablecloth. "If you're thinking something, just say it."

She met my gaze but still hesitated. Then she leaned forward, folding her hands on the table. "Listen, I'm here to support you. You're getting pulled in a hundred directions, and you have a ton on your plate. I don't want to add to that."

I raised my eyebrow. "But . . . ?"

"But I'm also worried about you. And about how you're handling everything. Especially tomorrow."

"I don't even know. I've just kind of been going through the motions because I don't know what else to do." I exhaled, hard. "To tell you the truth, I don't know what I'm doing. I've been a fucking wreck since the night it happened, and after that test turned positive . . ."

"I think anybody would be. Under both circumstances." She swallowed. "I'm not going to try to talk you out of it. It's your call. But at least promise me this *is* your call. Your choice. Not his."

I lowered my gaze.

"Kim . . ."

Rubbing the back of my neck, I sighed heavily. "I don't know what else to do. Like I said before, I can't put the baby up for adoption without his consent."

She swore under her breath.

I lifted my gaze. "All I can do now is get the abortion and then report the assault and hope to God it doesn't get swept under the rug."

"Damn." She pinched the bridge of her nose, then lowered her hand. "And so we're clear, I'm not judging you. I just hate the fact that he's making the call."

I scowled. "He's made all the decisions from the start."

"I know. And none of them are his to make."

"So what do you think I should do?"

Reese was quiet for a moment, then sighed. "I don't know. I really wish I had an alternative for you."

"Me too."

And once again, the waitress's timing was perfect. She set our plates and drinks down in front of us, and Reese and I shook off the uncomfortable conversation in favor of enjoying our meal.

There was something kind of strange about sitting out here, having a nice dinner above the beach just hours before . . . before go time. Like I should've been holed up in the cold motel room, freaking out instead of letting the sun warm my shoulders while I ate with Reese.

I was terrified. I was trapped. I was hurting, and tomorrow, I'd be hurting physically, too.

But at least I wasn't alone.

CHAPTER 10
REESE

We were in no hurry, but eventually, as the sun was getting lower in the clear sky, the waitress took our empty plates and left us with nearly dry drinks.

Kim drained her glass and set it down. "Should we head back to the hotel?"

I sighed. Tomorrow was going to start early. Might as well let her get as much sleep as she could. "Yeah, I guess."

Her features tightened, and she gazed out at the ocean again.

"We don't have to yet." I gestured down at the stretch of white sand, where only a few people still lingered. "We could go wander around on the beach for a little while. Looks like the tourists have mostly cleared out."

She seemed to ponder the idea for a moment. Then she shook some tension out of her shoulders and managed a slight smile. "That sounds really good. Let's go."

We split the bill, paid, and headed down to the beach.

A few steps in, Kim stopped. "Damn it."

"What?"

"Sand." She laughed as she took off her sandal. "You know how people write personal ads and say they love long walks on the beach?" She shook out the sand. "I think most of those people have never actually taken a long walk on the beach."

I laughed, too. "Don't you like it, though?"

"Of course." She took off her other sandal and shook the sand off it. "But I hate sand in my shoes."

"Yeah, me too." I toed off my own sandals. "Screw it. I'm going barefoot."

"Good idea." She looked around. "This isn't one of those beaches with broken glass and stuff on it, is it?"

"Better not be."

"Eh." She shrugged and hooked her fingers in the straps of her sandals. "I've had a tetanus shot."

"Me too. And if there's anthrax on anything, I'm good to go."

Kim laughed. Like, really laughed. "I *knew* those bastard shots would pay off eventually!"

I snorted. "Or maybe the ads should use that as a slogan: *Come to Waikiki—you won't even need the anthrax shot!*"

She smothered a giggle. "Oh yeah. That would get people here in droves."

"You never know. People visit places for the weirdest reasons."

Her amusement suddenly vanished, and my heart dropped.

"I . . . That's not what I meant."

"I know." She sighed and watched the tide rolling in. "One of these days, I would like to come back here just for a vacation."

"Yeah, me too. Someday, I'm going to hike Diamond Head." I nodded toward the huge rock formation in the distance. "I only had a couple of days when my ship came into Pearl Harbor."

"Maybe next time." She glanced at me. "We could always come back in a few months."

"Really? I mean, yeah. I'd love to. Isn't like it costs much to get here from Okinawa if we take a military flight."

"Then let's do it. Ditch the command for a little while and go up there." She gestured at Diamond Head. "The view must be incredible."

"No kidding. Have you ever been up on the castles on Okinawa?"

"No. I've driven past Katsuren, but I haven't been to any of them."

"Oh, you're missing out. The views are just spectacular."

"Yeah? Which one's your favorite?"

We continued down the beach, shoes in hand and warm wind in our hair, chatting about the places we'd visited—or wanted to visit—on Okinawa. All the while, I couldn't help stealing the odd glance at her. This was a side of Kim I'd never seen before. She was hours away from something I couldn't imagine going through, but she was relaxed right now, smiling and strolling down a beach with her sandals dangling from her fingers.

Even as we walked and talked, guilt gnawed at me for how I'd felt about her before. She wasn't one of the women who gave military women a bad name. It was men like Stanton and his ilk who gave us a bad name.

And Stanton, that son of a bitch, had put her in this situation and left her with few, if any, options. I wished she would cancel tomorrow, but it wasn't my choice to make. Even if Stanton had made it for her, that didn't make it my place to step in and tell her not to go through with it.

Especially since I still couldn't offer any alternatives. Stanton had her cornered, and he had our entire chain of command in his back pocket. With as much as he had to lose, I had no doubt he'd fight tooth and claw to make sure any action she took blew up in her face. Even if it only came out that Stanton had fathered her baby, regardless of whether it was consensual, he could be strung up for adultery, fraternization, and conduct unbecoming an officer and a gentleman. His career—and likely his marriage—would be over. There was no way in hell he'd let this destroy his life like that, and he had far more power and influence than Kim did.

She needed an ally with more clout than an MA2, and I couldn't find one for her. Stanton had his lips firmly around the dick of everyone above him, and everyone below him had *their* lips around *his*.

Even Alejandro. I cringed. There were times when I'd thought about telling him about what had happened to me, but after hearing him the other day . . .

There weren't many feelings worse than knowing you'd just lost one of your closest, most trusted allies.

But we didn't need to think about that or anything else tonight. Not with tomorrow creeping up way too fast and only a few hours between now and then for Kim to catch her breath and relax.

After we'd walked for a little while, Kim stopped. "I, um . . ." She faced me. "I wanted to say thanks, Reese. For coming out here." Her smile was slow to form, but when it did it was warm. "It really means a lot."

I returned the smile, trying not to get distracted by the way the setting sun played in her eyes and her dark hair. "You're welcome." I wrapped my arms around her. "And I promise, I'll be here for everything."

"Thank you."

I closed my eyes and held her tighter. "I know it doesn't seem like it right now, but it does get easier."

She hugged me back. "When?"

I swallowed, holding her tighter. "It just takes time. One day you wake up, and it doesn't own you quite as much as it did the day before."

"I thought I *was* getting better." She sighed heavily. "Then I missed my period, and . . ."

"I know." I stroked her hair. "I just wish there was more I could do."

She rested her head against my shoulder. "You've done way more than I could have asked anyone to." Kim raised her head, pulled back, and met my eyes. Hers were wet, but her smile was genuine. "I'm serious. I can't even tell you how much that means."

I smiled and brushed a few strands of windblown hair out of her face. "Nobody should have to go through anything like this alone."

Her expression turned more serious, her forehead creasing as she searched my eyes. "You did."

I flinched. "Doesn't mean you should."

"Thank you." She hugged me again, and I held her tight.

Goddamn, I hated not being able to shield her from all of this. I could tell her it got easier—and it did, slightly and slowly. I could make sure she was safe and taken care of tomorrow—and I would.

But Stanton had still raped her. Short of going back in time, there was no erasing this from her life.

I am so sorry you have to hurt like this, Kim.

After a moment, she wiped her eyes. "It's getting late. I guess we should get to the room."

I nodded. "Yeah. Let's go."

I kept an arm around her shoulders as we slowly headed toward the car. Tomorrow was going to be hell, and there was nothing I could do about that.

But at least she'd had this evening.

CHAPTER 11

KIM

There was only one other time in my life when I could remember my heart beating this hard. Ironically, it was the night I'd gotten pregnant in the first place.

I didn't bother trying to read a magazine. Sometimes I stared at the TV screen beside the receptionist's desk, but the news was on and it was depressing as always.

I glanced up, and my stomach flipped over. The clock on the wall had to be wrong. Was my appointment really in five minutes?

No, four minutes.

Oh fuck.

I closed my eyes and took a few slow, deep breaths. Within the hour, I'd be under sedation, and when I woke up, this would all be over.

Right?

Except the physical recovery. And going back to Okinawa. And facing Stanton again.

It's done, I could hear myself saying.

Good. Now we can forget this ever happened.

But I couldn't forget. Any of it. Not that night. Not the threats in his office.

Not . . . *this.*

A nurse appeared in the doorway. "Ms. Lockhoff?"

No turning back now. I stood and glanced at Reese. To the nurse, I said, "Can she come in with me?"

"Of course. She can stay with you while we're taking your vitals and prepping you for surgery."

My stomach lurched. Surgery. Fuck. Maybe I should've gone with the chemical version. I could've taken a pill and been done with it. Well, aside from the pain and recovery, but those were guaranteed either way. Somehow, when I'd scheduled this, the surgical option had been more appealing because I could be oblivious for the worst part. I hadn't considered how I'd feel walking back to pre-op, my legs shaking so bad I wasn't sure I could keep them under me. Reese stayed close, and with every step I had to stop myself from grabbing her arm and begging her to take me away from this place.

The nurse pushed open the exam-room door and gestured for me to go in. Reese took a seat. I eyed the exam table, which was more like a chair, sitting semi-upright.

"Sit right here, Ms. Lockhoff." The nurse patted the tissue paper–covered table-chair. "I'm just going to take your vitals, and then we'll have you change into a gown so we can get an IV started."

Oh God.

Stomach roiling and heart pounding, I sat on the edge of the chair while she wrote something in my chart. I caught Reese's eye, and she gave a reassuring, if slight, smile. I tried to return it, but as the nurse put her pen aside and turned to me again, I had to focus on not getting sick or passing out.

Was I really doing this?

I swallowed hard, and I felt Stanton's hand on my neck again, his thumb across my windpipe. *Just get it done.*

The nurse was talking to me, telling me what she was about to do, what would happen between now and the anesthesia kicking in. At least, that was what I thought she was saying. I nodded, answering automatically, but the only voice I heard was Stanton's.

If I'm the father, then I have paternal rights.

And I promise you, if you decide to nuke my life and career with this kid and this "rape" bullshit—

The nurse put a plastic ID bracelet around my wrist.

—I will exercise every one of those rights.

She slid a blood pressure cuff onto my arm, and as it constricted, I gripped the table's edge, focusing on that instead of the sensation of someone holding on to me. My arm, my throat . . .

Get it done*, MA3.*

The edges of my vision darkened, and the room shifted.

The nurse's hands appeared on my shoulders. "You okay, honey?"

"I just . . ." *I shouldn't be here.* "Got a little dizzy."

"That happens sometimes. Let's have you lie back a bit." She gestured behind me. "Just relax, honey." She moved her hand from my shoulder to my arm and pushed gently to guide me back against—

I was in the reclined passenger seat again. Streetlamps. Dashboard lights. Fingers digging into my arm. Someone shoving my skirt up to my hip.

"Just relax," a voice that might've been the nurse's and might've been Stanton's echoed in my ears. "Lie back."

Fighting didn't do any good against hands that strong. I couldn't get enough air. The world was spinning. I couldn't breathe. Where the fuck was I? In the car? In an exam room? Was that a dome light or a fluorescent? Where the—

"Kim." Reese's voice startled me back to the exam room. She cupped my face. "Look at me, Kim."

I blinked a few times until I focused on her and grabbed her wrist because I needed to touch her and be sure she was really there.

"Kim, you're safe." She stroked my hair with her other hand. "You're in the clinic. On Oahu. You're safe."

A shudder went through me, and I sank back against the half-reclined table. Cold water surged through my veins. My hand shook as I released Reese's wrist, and I tried to just breathe.

"You with me, Kim?"

I nodded. When had my whole body started shaking like this?

Reese turned her head. "Can we have a minute?"

"Sure. Of course." The nurse? Where had she come from? "I'll be right outside."

"Thank you." Reese faced me again. "Just breathe."

"I need to—"

"Breathe," she whispered. "You don't have to do anything until you're ready. Give yourself some time to come back down."

"What the hell happened?"

She stroked my face with soft fingertips. "I think you had a flashback."

I licked my dry lips. "God. I did." The tissue paper crinkled under me as I let my head rest on the pillow. "Jesus . . ."

She took my hand. "Has it passed?"

"I think so." I turned toward her. "Do they happen to you?"

Reese nodded. "Not so much anymore, but . . . yeah." Her thumb ran back and forth along mine. "They're terrifying, I know."

I rubbed my other hand over my face, wiping away sweat. "I don't even know what happened."

"Don't try to figure it out right now. Just let yourself relax."

I closed my eyes.

Reese squeezed my hand. "You don't have to go through with this, Kim."

"Yes, I do." I struggled to find my breath. "They can't get me in again before my leave is—"

"It's okay. You can always take more leave if you need to." She released my hand and touched my face again. The pad of her thumb made soft, comforting arcs along my cheekbone, and I focused on that as she whispered, "Once it's done, there's no going back. If you're not sure, then don't. There's still time to think it over."

I chewed my lip.

A quiet knock at the door turned both our heads. It opened slightly, and the nurse poked her head through. "Are you doing better, honey?"

I nodded. "Yeah. You can come in."

She shut the door behind her.

I took a breath. "I'm . . . I'm not sure I can go through with this."

The nurse set my chart on the counter. "A lot of young ladies do reconsider at the last minute. It's a big decision."

I swallowed the lump rising in my throat. "Except I need to do this."

She looked at me with kind eyes. "You're only eight weeks along. You still have time before the law becomes an issue." She took my hand and squeezed it gently. "It's an important decision, so if you want to use that time . . ."

I glanced at Reese, and she nodded.

The nurse touched my shoulder. "I'll give you a few minutes."

She left again. As soon as we were alone, Reese put her arm around my shoulders, and I almost broke down.

"I don't know what to do," I whispered.

"You heard the nurse." She smoothed my hair. "If you need more time, take it. This is *your* decision. No one else's. Definitely not *his*. Don't make it until you're absolutely sure you're ready."

"What about our leave?"

"We'll work it out. I'll email MA1. He'll make it happen. I promise."

I wasn't so sure Gutiérrez would grant us an extension, but I just hugged her back and murmured, "Thank you."

Stepping out of that cool, sterile air and into the thick humidity was beyond liberating. Everything had been out of my control since the night Stanton had raped me, but finally, I was the one making a decision.

Reese slid into the driver's seat, and as I buckled my seat belt, asked, "Where do you want to go?"

"Let's just go back to the room for now. I think I need to decompress."

"Sounds like a plan." She turned the key but didn't put the car in gear yet. "You're doing the right thing, by the way."

I met her eyes. "Do you think getting the abortion is the wrong thing?"

She chewed the inside of her cheek. "Not necessarily. And that's not my decision to make anyway. I meant giving yourself a little more time to make sure this is what you want."

I exhaled. "Hopefully a few days will be enough time to figure it out."

"Hopefully."

Neither of us talked on the way back to the motel. God knew what she was thinking about as she stared out at the road. Me, I just watched the scenery going by as I tried to sort out the jumble of thoughts banging around in my mind. I wanted to cry because this whole situation wouldn't go away. I wanted to laugh because it was all so damned absurd, and maybe if I laughed, I wouldn't cry. But the opposing needs seemed to cancel each other out, and I was just . . . numb. Exhausted. I was sure Reese was right and I'd done the right thing, and at the same time, I was equally convinced I'd just royally fucked up and this would come back and bite me in the ass.

Reese pulled into the motel parking lot, and we headed inside.

This room had felt like a prison cell for the last few days. I didn't have much money and hadn't been in the mood for doing touristy stuff by myself, so I'd spent almost the entire week cooped up in here, staring at the walls and wondering when the hell this would all be over.

But coming back to it now, I felt safe. Like walking through the door meant I'd really escaped, that no one would grab me and drag me back to the clinic to finish what I'd started.

No one was coming after me. They'd all been kind and supportive, though they'd advised me of the fees for canceling within twenty-four hours, and then I'd torn off the medical bracelet and headed for the door. No one had tried to stop me. Stanton's reach hadn't extended to the palm-shaded women's clinic on Oahu, and I'd signed myself out with no incident.

As Reese turned the dead bolt, I sank onto the foot of the bed, sitting on the same spot where I'd nearly broken down the other day. Right before I'd begged Reese for the support that had turned into a plane trip and her reassuring company.

She stepped away from the door and put a hand on my shoulder. "How are you holding up?"

"I'm okay." I released a breath. "And thanks. I guess I wasn't ready to go through with it."

"Then it's all right to wait." She went to her seabag and pulled out her laptop. "Let me email Gutiérrez before I forget."

"Are you sure he'll give us an extension on our leave?"

"He will if he knows what's good for him," she muttered. I couldn't decide if the implication was that he'd have to answer to Stanton or to her, but either way, as long as the extension was granted, I'd be happy.

She tapped out an email, sent it, and closed her laptop. "There. Done."

"And you're sure he'll—"

"He will. Trust me."

I sat back, resting my hands behind me. "Just another reason I'm glad you're here."

She smiled as she slid her laptop back into her bag. "I'm here to help."

"But I'm burning your leave."

She shrugged. "I've got forty days on the books."

"Still. You had to take leave, be at the terminal at 0200." I shook my head. "Why?"

She sat down beside me and took my hand in hers. "You said you needed someone."

I held her gaze and her hand but didn't say anything. The truth was, I hadn't just needed someone. Whether or not I'd realized it at the time, looking at her now, there wasn't a doubt in my mind—I'd needed *her*. I couldn't explain why, but out of the other seven billion people on this planet, I was grateful as hell to have this one in particular sitting here with me.

She laced our fingers together. "Maybe after we've chilled for a bit, we should go get you something to eat."

"Good idea. Now that you mention it, I'm starving." I shuddered at the memory of why I hadn't eaten since last night. "I could eat just about anything, I think."

"I don't doubt that at all." She stood, picked up the rental car's keys, and spun them around her finger. "Let's go."

CHAPTER 12

REESE

Hawaii had some amazing places to eat. Tons of cool varieties of ethnic foods.

So where did we go?

Burger King.

Maybe we were both just really, really hungry. I hadn't been able to eat this morning, and hadn't wanted to eat in front of her anyway, but now that she had a reprieve from the procedure, my stomach settled a bit. And we both agreed—greasy fast food sounded really fucking good.

We took the burgers to go and headed down to the beach. There, we spread a towel on the sand beneath a palm tree and sat with the food bags between us. For a long time, we just ate and watched the ocean, enjoying the warm afternoon.

It occurred to me that we were much more comfortable together than we'd been in the beginning. That she trusted me. And maybe that meant I owed her a little bit of honesty.

I broke the silence. "So, um." I picked at my fries. "When we met, I told you we had more in common than you probably thought."

Kim nodded. "Yeah."

"I couldn't talk about it that night, because . . ." I swallowed hard. "I haven't actually told anyone about it. Ever."

"I don't blame you."

I took a deep breath. "I should, though. And the mandated reporter thing, it . . . The statute of limitations is up, so it's a moot point."

"Noted. It stays between you and me then. You don't have to tell me, though." She lifted her eyebrows, asking without asking.

"You told me yours." I pulled my cigarettes and lighter out of my pocket. "Seems only fair I should tell you mine. If you, uh . . . if hearing it doesn't bother you."

"No, it's okay." Kim shifted beside me. "That whole *not being alone* thing."

"Gotcha. Just, if it bothers you say so, and I'll drop it."

"Okay."

Neither of us spoke as I took out a cigarette and lit it. I took a deep drag, praying that the nicotine got into my bloodstream before I started shaking. Even after all this time, I didn't like letting my mind go back to that dark place.

"It happened when I was in Afghanistan." I pulled my knees up to my chest, shrugging away a chill in spite of the hot breeze. "My LPO didn't like women in his unit to begin with, and everybody knew it. One night, we were transporting some detainees from our base to a transfer. Long story short, he made a bad call." I sighed and shook my head. "He wanted to get back to the base because it was almost the end of shift. And, I mean, it was hot as fuck. We were exhausted. But being hot and tired doesn't give you an excuse to cut corners when it comes to dealing with detainees."

"No, it doesn't." Kim wrinkled her nose. "And they put this guy in charge?"

Rolling my eyes, I gestured at the place on my arm where my insignia would've been if I'd been in uniform. "He had more chevrons than the rest of us. Whether we liked it or not, he was in charge."

"Ugh." She rolled her eyes too. "So . . . what happened?"

I took a breath. "He made a bad call, and I called him out on it. Normally I wouldn't do something like that, especially not in front of subordinates, but he was going to get us all killed. The assistant LPO backed him up, but everyone else thought I was right. And it turned out I *was* right. They'd been lazy about the pat down and missed a knife under a detainee's clothes." I shuddered. The desert sun glinting off that blade was a memory I'd carry with me until the day I died. "I mean, what if that had been a bomb, you know?"

"No kidding."

"So, of course, he got his ass chewed over it, and the assistant LPO did, too. They probably would've been hemmed up, but they both had buddies in the chain of command who swept the whole thing under the rug and just told them to keep their shit straight after that."

"Sounds familiar."

"Right?" I picked at the fries, my appetite suddenly gone, then took another drag instead. The chill under my skin was getting worse by the second. I hugged myself tighter and rested my chin on my knee. "So one night after chow, he and the assistant LPO pulled me aside and said they wanted to talk to me about it. I figured they were just going to give me hell about insubordination, but at least they had the good graces to do it in private. So I went with them."

Kim's hand went to her mouth, and her eyes widened.

I swallowed. "As soon as we were alone, my LPO grabbed me and told me if I made a sound, I was dead. And then they took turns. For . . . Shit, I don't even know how long it went on." I took a deep drag off my cigarette, wishing my nicotine tolerance wasn't so goddamned high these days. "And they kept telling me the whole time that this was my commendation for being a motherfucking hero."

"Jesus," she breathed. "I didn't realize it was two guys. I thought it was just one. Not that that's any better, just . . ."

"I think my LPO knew I'd have kicked his ass if he'd come at me alone," I growled.

"He was probably right." Her voice was little more than a hollow, horrified whisper.

"Oh, he was."

Kim pulled her knees up to her chest and wrapped her arms around them. "So, what happened to them?"

I tapped my cigarette over the sand. "Nothing."

"Nothing?"

"I never told anyone. Because I was scared." I turned to her. "For a lot of the same reasons you've been scared to turn in Stanton."

She shuddered when I said his name. "Do you ever regret it? Not reporting it?"

"I wish I could have, and I wish I'd gotten them both strung up." I shifted my gaze back out to the ocean. "But I don't know what good it would've done if I *had* reported it. There was a woman on the base who tried to nail a sergeant for sexual assault, but the investigation never got off the ground. And she ended up getting out at twelve years because she couldn't deal with the environment anymore."

"I can understand that."

"Yeah. Me too." I tapped my cigarette over the sand again. "That's the whole reason I started smoking. When I first went to Afghanistan, I could *almost* deal with the stress, but after what happened? Especially when I still had to work for those fuckers every damned day for another five months?" I shook my head. "I needed something to help."

"And people wonder why Sailors drink."

"If they wonder, they aren't paying attention." I extinguished the cigarette and dropped the butt into my mostly empty soda cup. Going back to that time had left me jittery, so I didn't even try to talk myself out of lighting up another. After I'd taken a drag off the fresh cigarette, I said, "The worst part is knowing the LPO is still in the Navy. Last I heard, he made board for chief."

Kim's jaw dropped. "No way."

"And the best part? Right before I transferred here, he got to put on gold stripes." Bitterness seeped into my voice as I added through my teeth, "For twelve years of good fucking conduct."

"Jesus Christ."

"That's what I said."

"What about the other one? The assistant LPO? Did he get out?"

I blew out some smoke. "He's dead."

"He's . . ." Kim blinked. "Really?"

"Yep. When they . . . When the incident happened, he was there on his fourth tour in six years—two in Afghanistan and two in Iraq— and he already had some serious PTSD by that point." I took a drag and slowly exhaled the smoke. "Couple of months after he went home, he ate his service weapon."

"Wow. I don't know if that's sad or poetic."

"A little of both." I crushed my cigarette and wrapped my arms around my knees again. "It's weird. Part of me thinks *good riddance*, but part of me . . ."

Kim put her hand on my arm. "What?"

I took a breath. "The thing is, the LPO was a fucking sociopath. All the women were nervous around him anyway, and everyone thought he was a bit unhinged. That was his first combat tour, though. He'd been deployed as part of ship's company before that but never in the desert. Whatever was wrong with him, it had nothing to do with the war." I was nauseated just thinking about that asshole.

He'd given me the creeps long before he'd torn my uniform in that stuffy office. "But the assistant . . . I just can't help but wonder if he was messed up in the head from spending four years of his life over there. Not that it excuses anything, and I would've been happy as fuck to see him wind up in the brig for what he did to me, I just . . ." How the hell was I supposed to word that? Especially to a woman who'd been raped, too?

Kim squeezed my arm. "You wonder if the guy who raped you was really him or if it was what going to war turned him into?"

"Yes. Exactly. I mean, would he have done anything like that if he hadn't been so messed up from combat? It's like, I would never excuse the guys who go home and kill their families, either, but . . . I kind of get it. Being over there, it . . . does things to you. Changes you." I looked her in the eyes. "I don't care what anyone says, no one comes back the same person they were when they left." I picked up my wrinkled pack of cigarettes. "I came back a smoker. Alejandro started doing dip after he went to Gitmo, so—"

"Alejandro?"

I tensed. "MA1 Gutiérrez, I mean."

She furrowed her brow. "You guys are on a first name basis?"

"We go back a ways. We met in 'A' school, when we were still the same rank. Sometimes it's hard to remember he's my LPO now." *Lately, it's hard to remember he's my friend.* "This is the first time we've been stationed together since school, but we've stayed in touch for years." *Somehow I doubt that's going to last.*

Kim wadded up her burger wrapper and stuffed it into the empty bag. "So, how many tours have you done in the Sandbox?"

I held up two fingers. "I went to Iraq during my first enlistment and Afghanistan a couple of years later. Iraq wasn't too bad. I was stationed in one of the bases that didn't see a lot of action, so I was mostly standing around with a rifle while the Army guys rebuilt schools and shit."

"And Afghanistan?" Kim hesitated. "I mean, besides what happened with your LPO?"

"Afghanistan was hell. We were in a bad spot. Lots of . . ." I swallowed the queasiness. "It was a really active area, let's put it that way."

"Wow. Dealing with that and what those guys did, I can't even imagine."

"I've done okay, all things considered. I saw a lot of shit I'll never be able to forget, and I'm a little more familiar than I'd like to be with getting too close to IEDs and enemy fire, but I've done all right. Nightmares now and then, but that's about it. I don't have constant flashbacks and stuff like some of the others in my unit." I held up my cigarette. "Mostly I just have these."

"I can understand that." She paused. "Thanks. For telling me. I know it's rough to relive that kind of thing."

"Actually, it's . . ." I wrapped my arms around my bent knees. "I've never talked about it before. It's kind of nice to get it out. And . . ." I glanced at her, some heat rushing into my cheeks. "It's good to tell it to someone who believes me."

Kim put her hand on my arm and squeezed. "I believe you. And I know you believe me, too."

We held each other's gaze. Some of the guilt that had taken up residence in my chest finally started to dissipate—maybe Kim and I hadn't gotten off on the right foot, but we'd reached an understanding. We'd found some trust that I hadn't even realized I'd been missing in my life. And as far as I could tell, she'd forgiven me for our rough beginning. Thank God.

Kim drew her hand back and cleared her throat. "So, you said you know Gutiérrez?"

I nodded.

"But you don't think he'd help me?"

I brushed a few strands of hair out of my face and gazed out at the ocean because I couldn't look her in the eye anymore. "Up until recently, he'd have been the first person I'd have gone to. But now . . ."

"What happened?"

I chewed the inside of my cheek. "I, um, overheard some things. Apparently he's friendlier with Stanton than I thought."

Kim sighed. "I really don't have any allies, do I?"

I took her hand and met her eyes. "You have me."

I was afraid she'd scowl and remind me that there wasn't a damned thing I could do for her. That I was as powerless as she was.

But she squeezed my hand and smiled. "Thank you. You've been amazing through all of this."

I returned the smile and hugged her.

But what I wouldn't have given for the power to make this whole thing go away.

CHAPTER 13
KIM

We went back down to Waikiki that afternoon to relax and unwind. A few blocks from the beach, we wandered through shop after shop of Hawaiian-themed merchandise. Some were quite nice—we spent almost half an hour drooling over amazing hand-carved wooden statues in one shop. Of course we couldn't have afforded any of them, but they sure were pretty to look at. Some of the other shops, though, were obviously geared toward those who either had horrible taste or still wanted souvenirs after they'd spent most of their money on hotels and maitais.

After checking out some gorgeous seascape paintings, we strolled into another shop full of touristy crap.

I wrinkled my nose and picked up a hideous picture frame made out of plastic hibiscus flowers. "Do people actually put stuff like this out in their houses?"

"I think they buy them for people they don't like."

"Oh, that would explain it." I gestured with the frame. "If I got a gift like this? Message received."

She snickered. "What about this one?" She held up a cheap sculpture of a colorful tropical fish.

I giggled. "If someone gave me that, I would unfriend the crap out of them."

"But Kim"—she batted her eyes and pretended to pet the fish—"it's the thought that counts, right?"

"Mm-hmm. Exactly."

She laughed and set it back on the shelf. "This looks like the kind of weird shit you can find on Kokusai Street."

"Really? I've never been there."

"You've been on Okinawa for six months, and you've never been down to Kokusai Street?" She smiled. "You should check it out. It's got a lot of touristy stuff, but you can find some really cool pottery and glass there."

"Really?" I started to speak, hesitated, then decided to hell with it. "When we get back to the island, could you show me around?"

Reese's smile turned to a grin. "I will show you *all* the cool places. Including the ones nobody knows about."

"Promise?"

She held up a fist with her pinky extended. I hooked mine in hers, and we exchanged grins. My God, it had been so long since I'd done this. Goofing around.Shopping.Giggling.Having a few fruity drinks, even if they were virgin. I'd been lonely as hell for the last few years but hadn't realized just how much I'd missed *this*.

We continued through the store, past the weird trinkets and into the racks of Hawaiian shirts, bikinis, and brightly colored dresses.

"Hey, Kim. What do you think?" Reese picked up the most hideous flowery dress I'd ever seen and held it up in front of herself. "Should I get this for the Navy Ball?"

I snorted. "I dare you."

She smothered a laugh. "Really? I totally will."

"Except then you'd have to actually go to the Navy Ball."

"Oh. Right." She hung it up again. "Fuck that. I'd rather—oh my God! Did you see these?" She grabbed a pair of sunglasses that had thick rims made out of cowrie shells and put them on. Striking a pose, she said, "Should I buy them?"

I snickered. "You totally should. They're so you."

"Hey!"

"You asked."

"Okay, I did." She put them back on the rack. "But I have too many sunglasses as it is, so . . . no."

"Whatever helps you sleep at night, darling."

We both laughed and headed out of the shop and back into the warm afternoon. As we stepped outside, moving from fluorescent light to the bright tropical sun, I glanced at Reese, and my breath caught.

Oh yeah. *That* was why I'd had a crush on her when I'd first checked into the command, even though our uniforms had never been accused of being particularly flattering. They made the guys look great, but somehow managed to completely flatten our butts and boobs. Even dressed like that, with some of her best features covered up by blue camouflage, she'd been hot.

In a T-shirt and shorts, though? Reese was *smoking* hot. She had the kind of hips and ass that made my mouth water, and her intense PT sessions definitely showed—with arms like that it was no wonder she could take down belligerent suspects without much trouble.

Out here, out of uniform, away from everybody else's bullshit, she looked amazing. Dressed down and relaxed with her brown hair pulled back into a messy ponytail instead of the rigid bun she wore to work and that playful smile on her lips, she made my heart stop every time she looked at me.

Like she was doing right now.

I cleared my throat as heat rushed into my cheeks. "Sorry, what?"

She cocked her head but didn't press. "I was just asking if you wanted to keep going through shops or maybe go down to the beach?"

"Uh." I glanced around. The sidewalks were getting crowded as the sun was starting to go down. "How about the beach?"

She grinned. "Want to get some more sand in your shoes?"

"No, ma'am. I plan to take them off this time. *Before* that happens."

Reese winked. "Smart."

We both laughed and headed toward the strip of high-rise hotels that stood along the beach. As we did, I stole a few more glances at her.

This was the woman I'd thought was a complete and total bitch?

After spending time with this side of Reese, I felt like a jerk for ever thinking what I had about her. Truth was, she was exactly the way I'd been at my last command. And what had I done? Stopped just short of calling *her* Razor Wire.

But that wasn't her. Not even close. She was completely different here. Hell, we both were. Half an ocean away from our fucked-up command, for the first time since I'd joined the Navy, I got to have a normal evening with a girl. I'd almost forgotten what that was like.

And I'd definitely forgotten what it was like to lose my breath every time that girl looked my way.

Question was, did she feel the same?

I quickly banished that thought. Reese had come here to help me when I'd been about to lose my mind. That didn't mean there was any more to this.

At least I had a friend now.

But did I dare imagine she could be something more?

CHAPTER 14
REESE

We stopped for a couple of virgin daiquiris on the way down to the beach, which staved off the lingering heat of the day. At the edge of the sand, we finished our drinks, then took off our sandals and made our way out onto the beach. The sand was hot but not enough to burn, and the tourists were steadily wandering back to the hotels, so everything was perfect. Not too crowded, not too hot—*perfect*.

Part of me was still reeling from finally telling someone what had happened to me in Afghanistan, but I also felt . . . freer. As if talking about it—or more to the point, having someone I could trust with it—was the key to letting it go. Obviously it would never go away completely, but I'd shaken it off enough that I could embrace this relaxing day out. Especially since I was spending it with . . .

Her.

The woman who'd let me unload my story even while she carried the weight of her own assault. In spite of the rocky start, we'd gotten to this place—trusting, comfortable—and I was so, so grateful. I was also keenly aware of my responsibility to support her emotionally right now.

A ways down the beach, Kim exhaled. "God, I needed this tonight."

"I'll bet you did."

She tilted her head to one side, then the other. "You'd think I would've thought to get out and relax a bit."

"Glad it's helping now."

"It is." She inhaled deeply, and as she let that breath go, a smile slowly formed on her lips. "So much."

"Good. How, um, how are you feeling? About everything?"

"You mean about bailing this morning?"

I shrugged. "Sure."

"I don't know. Part of me still wants to get it over with. Part of me doesn't know, well, anything."

"Well, at least now you have some time to catch your breath and think things over."

"Thank God." She turned to me. "Or, well, I guess I should say thank *you*."

I smiled. "No, it was your decision."

"Yeah, but I think I needed someone to talk me off the ledge and tell me that decision was okay." She rolled her eyes, her cheeks coloring. "Fuck. I sound like such an idiot. I swear, I can make my own decisions and think for myself, I've just been such a damned mess lately."

"Kim." I stopped, and when she did, too, I squeezed her shoulder. "Nobody expects you to have a completely clear head right now. Anyone who does is either clueless or an asshole. It's okay to lean on people."

"That's a tough thing to do when you're not used to being *able* to lean on anybody."

"Well, get used to it."

She hesitated but then returned the smile, and some of the tightness in her neck and shoulders seemed to disappear.

I didn't know what else to say. All I knew was I couldn't take my eyes off her. Fatigue and stress still made themselves known in the dark circles under her eyes, but the fading daylight played on her skin, filling in the color that exhaustion had taken away. Her blue eyes shone with more life than they had before. She still had a long way to go, but it was like she had her spark back, even if it was only for tonight.

Why would you do this to her, Stanton? Who in his right mind would break this girl?

Twin crevices deepened between her eyebrows. "What?"

"Hmm?"

"You were looking at me kind of, I don't know . . ."

"Oh. Sorry."

"What's wrong?"

"Nothing. I just . . ." I hesitated. "Okay, can I be totally honest about something?"

She shrugged. "Sure. Yeah."

"You've been different ever since I got here."

Kim scowled. "Wouldn't you be?"

"No, that's not what I mean. I don't mean it as a bad thing." I swept my tongue across my lips, catching the taste of my daiquiri and caught myself wondering if hers tasted the same. "I mean, you're dressed differently. Less"—I gestured at my face—"makeup."

"Oh." Her cheeks colored, and she turned toward the water. "Just didn't . . . didn't feel the need—"

"I like it."

Kim straightened, her lips parting. "What?"

"You're so much prettier like this. The real you."

"Really?"

I nodded. "I mean, I'm not saying you're not pretty the rest of the time, but like this, you're . . ." I exhaled. "Kim, you're stunning like this."

She smiled shyly. "Thanks." She gestured at herself. "It's funny. This is how I prefer to dress, but the other way, I thought that's how the guys liked girls."

I wrinkled my nose. "Fuck those guys. You don't need to please them."

"So I've learned," she whispered.

"I'm serious. What they think doesn't matter." As I spoke, I couldn't resist touching her face. She closed her eyes and released a breath but didn't recoil from my fingertips, so I gently rested my entire hand against her cheek. She pressed into it, her soft skin warm beneath mine.

I swallowed. "Is this okay?"

"Yeah." She put her hand over mine and looked up at me. "To be honest, aside from this trip, I haven't been touched by another girl since before I came to Okinawa."

"Neither have I."

Kim held my gaze. "How long ago was that?"

"Almost two years."

"Wow. That's a long time."

"Yeah. It is."

She ran her fingers through my hair. Gazing into her eyes, I wondered if her heart was beating as fast as mine.

The silence lingered. I kept searching for some way to fill it, but I couldn't think. Not when her gaze kept flicking back and forth from my eyes to my lips. Or when mine kept doing the same, alternating between her beautiful eyes and her parted lips.

Kim took a breath. Then she lifted her chin, and as if drawn by some unseen force, my body reacted to hers, moving in closer and leaning down until our lips almost brushed.

"Are you sure about this?" I whispered.

"I'm not sure about anything."

But she kissed me anyway.

Neither of us moved at first. My heart was beating out of control, but otherwise, I was as still as she was. Then she nudged my lower lip with hers, and I tilted my head slightly as I did the same to her.

My sandals slipped from my fingers and fell, forgotten, to the sand. A second later, hers fell, too. She parted her lips, and I parted mine, and as we wrapped our arms around each other, the kiss deepened.

Electricity shot right through me, and at the same time a lump rose in my throat. Jesus Christ, had I really gone so long without tasting another woman like this? Without *feeling* another woman?

I slid my hands down her sides, tracing the delicious curve of her waist as I drew her body closer to mine. Some people just fit together, every curve and angle fitting like they were made to, and Kim and I fit perfectly.

I ran my hand up again, but as I started over the swell of her breast, I pulled back.

She grabbed my wrist. "Don't."

"But I—"

She gently laid my hand back on her breast. "Please."

Then her lips were over mine again and we were kissing, and when I ran my thumb over her nipple, she moaned into my kiss and pressed against me.

"You sure this is okay?" I whispered.

"I feel like it shouldn't be." She drew back so we could see each other. "Seems like I shouldn't *want* to go any further." She ran her tongue across her lower lip. "But it's been so long since anything's felt good..."

I trailed my fingertips down the side of her face. "We can always stop."

"I don't want to." Swallowing hard, she met my eyes. "M-maybe we should go back to the room."

I shivered. "Yeah. Maybe we should."

CHAPTER 15
KIM

The drive back from Waikiki to our shithole motel took *forever*. After a red light lasted way longer than it should have, and the subsequent green light went by way too fast, I was tempted to suggest a beach or another hotel or *something* before I went out of my mind.

But finally, we made it, and my heart sped up as Reese pulled into a parking spot in front of the motel. We hurried from the car out into the hot evening air and through the door into the cool room.

Reese closed the door behind us and leaned against it. I faced her. Neither of us moved. Neither of us spoke. For what felt like hours, I couldn't look anywhere but right into her eyes.

She swallowed. So did I.

"You, um . . ." She cleared her throat. "You having any second thoughts?"

"No. You?"

She shook her head.

Knees shaking and heart pounding, I crossed the strip of space between us, but just before we touched, I lost my nerve. We were so close, not even an inch apart. If one of us leaned in even a little, we'd be kissing, but I . . . and she . . .

"I thought you weren't having second thoughts," she whispered unsteadily.

"Not second thoughts." I licked my lips. "Just nerves."

"That makes two of us." She lowered her gaze for a second. "How about this? If either of us is awkward or slow on the uptake, we'll just run with it. No judging, no laughing." She grinned cautiously. "What do you think?"

I held up my fist with my pinky extended. "Promise?"

Reese laughed and hooked her pinky in mine. "Promise."

We giggled, and some of the tension in the room dissipated. The moment passed, though, and our humor faded. We hadn't let go of each other's hand yet.

Holding her gaze, I touched her face, and we both shivered. She ran the backs of her fingers down my cheek.

"No judging," she whispered, still holding on to my pinky with her other hand. "We're both new to each other. I don't care if we're perfect."

"I don't, either." *I'm just scared of . . .*

To hell with it. Everything I was afraid of existed outside of this room, and everything I wanted was standing right in front of me, so I used my grip on her pinky to pull us together and I kissed her.

Reese let go of my hand, and we wrapped our arms around each other. Forget nerves. Forget second thoughts. Up until tonight, I'd gotten used to a lack of human contact, but now that I'd crossed a line and let myself kiss and touch her, I wanted more. I wanted to touch her all over. To be touched all over. I didn't care where this was going as long as we didn't stop.

I pressed against her, and she pulled me closer. The damned AC in this room kept the air way too cold, but that only made the warmth of Reese's body that much more addictive.

Without breaking the kiss, she nudged me back a step. Then another. I let her guide me backward until my calves met the bed, and then we both sank onto the mattress.

She drew back a little, meeting my eyes. Her forehead creased, and she swallowed.

I caressed her face. "What's wrong?"

"Nothing. I just . . . This is the first time I've . . ." She closed her eyes. "Since what happened."

I tucked her hair behind her ear. "Me too."

Reese met my eyes again. "If we're going too fast, we can always stop."

I shook my head. "I don't want to stop. Do you?"

"Not a chance."

"Good." I ran my hands down her sides. "I'm not letting that son of a bitch control this part of my life, too."

She grinned. "That's my girl," and kissed me.

And suddenly this was more than kissing, more than touching. Nothing physical had changed, but somehow acknowledging we wanted this to go on had turned an inkling of arousal into something much bigger. We were still fully dressed, but I was in way, way over my head, and all I could think was more, more, *more.*

I slid my hands under her shirt, and we both gasped as bare skin met bare skin.

God. Yes. *More.*

As if reading my mind, she sat up, and I pushed her shirt up over her head. Just as I expected, she was beautiful. Slim but curvy, and—

That was a surprise. Sailors and ink went together like Sailors and swearing, but I hadn't expected Reese to have tattoos. Now that her shirt was off, two were visible, though one was obscured by her bra strap on the side of her rib cage.

On her upper arm, she had a master-at-arms eagle, and below it were three sets of initials, each with two dates beneath them. The end dates on all three were within two months of each other. She'd been to combat—I didn't have to ask what a tattoo like that meant, and I definitely wasn't going to ask in bed.

I ran a fingertip over the visible part of the other tattoo. "I want to see the rest of it."

"Is that a polite way of saying you want me to take off my bra?"

I batted my eyes. "Is it working?"

Reese didn't answer. She just reached back, unsnapped her bra, and tossed it aside.

For a moment, I forgot she even had tattoos. She was just . . . breathtaking. I couldn't resist touching her, running my hands over her perfectly proportioned breasts and hard nipples.

Finally, I remembered the tattoo that had been partially covered and tilted my head to get a better look. It was a colorful sun with a smiling face, each tendril painstakingly detailed in red, orange, and yellow.

I traced the edge of the design. "I didn't even realize you had any."

She grinned. "Every girl's got her secrets."

I returned the grin. "You have any more?"

"Maybe." She leaned in and kissed me again. "You'll just have to see, won't you?"

"Mm-hmm."

"And I showed you mine . . ."

"So I should show you mine?"

"You don't have to. But I would love to see."

"My tattoos?"

"You." She kissed me again. "*All* of you."

"Well, when you put it like that . . ."

We separated and shed our clothes. I caught a glimpse of another tattoo on her hip, and she glanced at the one on my shoulder, but neither of us stopped for a longer look. She drew me in for another kiss. Her lips were so soft and gentle. I loved the way her hair felt between my fingers and the way her hands roamed my waist and hips, pressing in just enough to let me know how turned on she was.

She pinched my nipple, and I whimpered. "Holy fuck . . ."

"This okay?"

"Yeah. They're just . . . really sensitive. *Really* sensitive."

"Does it hurt?"

"Mm-hmm." I put my hand over hers and squeezed, encouraged her to pinch it harder. "But it feels good."

"Good." She teased them some more, with her fingers and her lips and teeth, and just as it became too intense, she started kissing her way up. And then she was on top of me, and we were wrapped up in each other, naked, kissing, nothing between us. I couldn't remember ever being this aroused in my life.

A shiver went through me, but her body weight over mine kept me mostly still.

Immobile.

The next shiver wasn't quite so pleasant. Reese had a few inches on me. She was easily stronger than I was. If she wanted . . .

She pushed herself up and met my eyes. "You okay? You tensed up."

"I'm . . ." I moistened my lips.

"We don't have to." She cupped my face with a gentle hand. "We can stop if—"

"No." I ran my fingers through her long hair. "I don't want to stop."

"Let's just go slow, then," she whispered. "I think we both need it that way."

I nodded. "Slow is good. Maybe on our sides."

"Okay." She rolled over, drawing me with her. "Anytime you want to we can stop."

"Likewise."

But I didn't want to stop, and her touch said she didn't, either.

We settled onto our sides and pulled each other into another warm embrace. Not only could I move now, but Reese didn't have to hold herself up anymore. I rested my head on her arm, and her hand gently grasped my shoulder from behind. The other was completely free, and she took full advantage. I swore there wasn't an inch of skin she didn't caress.

The last time I'd had someone's hands on me, it had been rough and terrifying, every touch making me sick to my stomach. Deep down, fear lingered, ready to come to the surface and send me crashing back into that night.

But the longer we held each other, exploring naked skin and kissing like we could do this forever, the more my tense muscles relaxed. With every brush of skin or lips, that fear settled. The only nerves that stayed near the surface now were the ones that came with the territory of being with someone new—excitement, the need to do everything right, the fear of being unable to please her.

More than once, my mind tried to go back to that dark, dark place, but all I had to do was open my eyes and drink in Reese's soft curves and distinctive tattoos, and I knew this was her, not him. Everything was okay. More than okay.

Reese's fingertips grazed the places where he'd gripped me, and though the ghost of his touch was there, her gentleness was like an anchor, keeping me in the present.

I hadn't felt even a little bit horny in months, but now I wanted this. Bad. The demons in my head couldn't ruin tonight no matter how hard they tried. After all this time without being with a woman, and after what had happened with Stanton, I craved this. The gentleness, the mutual desire, the warmth of skin on skin. I'd almost forgotten what it felt like to surrender to the need for another woman and the pleasure we could give each other.

But, my God, I remembered now.

I pushed Reese onto her back and kissed my way down to her collarbone. I met her eyes as I took her nipple between my lips and when I pressed my teeth in just enough to make her gasp. Holding her nipple between my teeth, I teased it with my tongue.

"Holy shit . . ." She stroked my hair, her hand pausing now and again, and her fingers twitching like they were *just* about to grab on. "Fuck. *Fuck*, that's good."

I grinned and then continued downward, and as I kissed my way past her navel, she parted her legs. She might've whispered a curse into the otherwise silent room, but for all I knew, it was my own heartbeat spelling out my desire for her.

As I settled between her thighs, I wrapped an arm around each one, resting my hands on her hips to hold her steady.

And then I went down on her.

And almost lost my ever-loving mind.

God, I hadn't tasted pussy in so long, and the sweet tanginess of hers made my head spin. I took my time, not willing to rush this at all. Reese was *clearly* cursing now—she *was* a Sailor, after all—and kneading my scalp while I explored her like I'd never done this before. I traced the edges of her pussy lips and then marveled at the way her clit felt against my tongue.

"Oh fuck," she whimpered. "You are so . . . good at . . ."

I shifted onto one arm, keeping the other firmly over her hip to hold her still, and slipped two fingers inside her. Reese shivered and squirmed, cursed, gasped, cried out. Even as my tongue and jaw were starting to ache from the constant motion, I didn't stop. Not until she'd come. And, fuck, she felt like she was close.

She gasped, and her whole body tensed.

But . . .

Her gasp sounded more like she was startled, the tension in her body signaling alarm, not arousal.

Something wasn't right.

I lifted my head. Her eyes were still closed, her lips still taut, but . . . different. Like she was closer to a grimace than anything pleasurable.

I gently slipped my fingers free and pushed myself up over her so we were face-to-face. "Hey. What's wrong?"

Rubbing a hand over her face, she swallowed hard. "I'm . . . Nothing." She shook her head. "I'm okay."

I raised my eyebrows.

She lifted her head to kiss me. "I'm fine. And I loved what you were doing." She licked her lips. "Do it again. Please."

"Are you—"

"Please," she whispered. "I'm okay."

I hesitated, but she kissed me again and repeated, "Seriously. I'm okay."

So I didn't argue with her. I went down on her again, keeping her still with one arm over her hips. I slid my fingers back inside her, crooked them, and Reese moaned. She tried to buck against me, but I held her in place.

As I teased her clit with my lips and tongue and slowly fucked her with my fingers, I glanced up at her. My God, she was gorgeous. Her skin was starting to flush, especially her face and neck, and the way she bit her lip and screwed her eyes shut and arched and writhed . . . I could've watched her do that all night long. I could've *made* her do that all night long.

She pinched her nipples and squirmed, moaning as I kept teasing her. Her pussy tightened around my fingers, and she swore and gasped as I—

Her body tensed up again.

My heart skipped. I glanced at her and was about to lift my head to ask if she was all right, but she grabbed my hair. "D-don't stop."

I hesitated—*was* she all right?—but didn't stop. I licked her clit, finger-fucked her, everything I hoped she liked, and her moans and whimpers were made of pure pleasure.

"Don't stop, baby. Don't stop doing . . . doing that . . . just like that . . ." She gasped for breath, gripping my hair so hard it stung. "Holy shit, baby! Oh, fuck . . ."

I sped up *just* a little.

"Oh my God!" She tensed, her pussy clenching around my fingers, and I kept circling her clit with my tongue until she whimpered and nudged my head away.

She collapsed back onto the mattress. I carefully withdrew my fingers, lifted myself onto my arms and crawled up to kiss her. I was barely even over her before she threw her arms around me and pulled me down to her. She kissed me hard, her body still shaking under mine.

When I came up for air, I met her eyes, and my heart stopped. "What's wrong?" I brushed a tear off her cheek. "Are you okay?"

She nodded, smiling as she wiped her eyes. "Yeah."

"Are you sure?" My heart pounded. "I didn't—"

"It's okay." She wrapped her arms around me and held me, naked skin resting against naked skin. "Everything's okay." Her lips met mine, and there was no hesitation in her kiss, no reluctance or fear. I still didn't understand why she'd teared up like that, but I *did* understand that she hadn't wanted to stop.

"I can't even remember the last time I came so hard." She stroked my hair. "You're amazing."

I grinned. "Then I haven't lost my touch?"

"If you have, I want to be there when you get it back, because holy *fuck*." She didn't give me a chance to respond before she kissed me again, and any witty retort I might've had was gone the second our lips met.

She slipped her hand between my legs. I parted them for her, hungry for her touch, and moaned into her kiss as her fingertips teased my pussy lips. When I pressed back, trying to get her to the area that desperately needed attention, she laughed softly and drew a featherlight line around—but without touching—my clit.

"You're evil," I murmured.

"Mm-hmm. I am. But you—"

"Please, Reese." My back arched, which pressed my pussy against her fingers and my breasts against hers, and it didn't do a damned thing to relieve any of this tension. "I want . . . I want to come."

"Do you?"

"*Please.*"

"Well, since you asked nicely . . ."

I tried to speak but couldn't, because she'd found the most delicious rhythm, two fingers circling slowly and gently with my clit between them. As she did, she nudged me, and I didn't resist, letting her push me onto my back. She wasn't on top of me this time, instead lying beside me, and she kissed my neck as she kept on circling my clit and turning my entire body into liquid.

I pushed against her hand again, rocking my hips to complement the way her fingers moved, and between her kiss and her touch, I was in heaven. She teased me, and I ran my hands all over her body—her flat stomach, her gorgeous breasts, her beautifully curving waist. Fuck, everything about her was a turn-on. Her body. Her kiss. Her touch.

Her fingers moved faster. Faster. *Holy shit . . .*

My breath caught. My whole body felt like it was about to melt, or shatter, or somehow do both at the same time. My vision went white.

And then I came.

And I knew why she'd cried.

Release. Pure, foundation-rattling release. Nearly all the tension I'd been carrying broke free at once, and the rest was shaken free by the electricity coursing through my veins. I was flying, trembling, coming apart at the seams and loving every goddamned second of it.

Little by little, Reese backed off, and my orgasm tapered. I slowly came back down, settling to earth beside her, and the exhilarating sensation lingered.

Our surroundings came back into existence like a developing Polaroid. The bed. The four walls. Hawaii on the outside. All the reasons we were here to begin with.

But even as the familiar sick feeling crept back in, I felt better than I had in a long time. Liberated in some small but weirdly significant way.

It was as if all the demons in my head had been, if only for a few breathless seconds, silenced. They were still there, of course. Maybe one or two had been exorcised, but the rest had just temporarily shut the fuck up. Those few seconds of silence had taken a massive weight off my shoulders. The demons weren't gone. They wouldn't magically disappear. Some wouldn't go away anytime soon, some probably wouldn't go away at all.

But for the first time, I had an inkling of hope that they *might* go away.

The room was starting to get uncomfortably cool, so we pulled the sheet up over us and kept right on kissing and touching. Even just lying here like this, lazily making out under a rough hotel sheet, felt amazing. Like I could finally touch someone without breaking down, and someone was still willing to touch me without hurting me.

After a while, I moistened my lips. "Is it wrong that I already want to do it again?"

Reese propped herself up on her arm. "If that's wrong, I don't want to be right."

I laughed, running my fingers through her disheveled hair. "Don't you need to go out and have a cigarette?"

Reese shook her head. "No. I'm good."

"You don't smoke after sex?"

"No. I only smoke for stress relief. After sex is . . ." She smiled and caressed my face. "Well, after everything we just did, I don't really need to relieve any stress, do I?"

I grinned. "I guess you don't."

CHAPTER 16
REESE

Kim cuddled up next to me with her head on my shoulder, and for the longest time we just lay there in each other's arms beneath the covers.

I couldn't remember the last time I'd felt like this. This postcoital *sigh* feeling had been a stranger for quite a while.

I'd never had more cathartic sex in my life, and my emotions were running a million miles an hour in a million different directions. I wanted to laugh out loud. I wanted to cry. I wanted to hold on to her and never let go. I wanted to be sick.

That cigarette suddenly seemed more necessary than I'd thought, but I held off. A hit of nicotine sounded absolutely heavenly, but not quite as good as lying here beside Kim. Even if lying here beside Kim was part of the problem.

Jesus fuck. I'm going crazy, aren't I?

Closing my eyes, I kissed the top of Kim's head and ran my fingers up and down her back, all the while telling myself that I was okay. Nothing bad had happened, no matter how much I'd convinced myself it would.

Nevertheless, even while I'd been caught up in her, they'd been there. Not touching me—neither of them had been that gentle—but *there.* Waiting in the wings to take over and turn this amazing night into something hellish.

I fucking hated that feeling. For about a year after it happened, I'd been afraid to look over my shoulder—even more afraid not to—because I was sure they'd be there. Eventually, I'd shaken that off, but tonight, it had been back. As I'd tried to lose myself in Kim, there'd been that steadily growing certainty in the back of my mind that if I'd opened my eyes, she'd be gone and I'd be back in that makeshift office inside an under-ventilated, overheated shipping container. Held down, powerless, terrified.

The memory sent a shiver through me.

Kim lifted herself up and met my eyes. "You okay?"

I nodded. "Are you?"

"Yeah, I'm good." A slight smile played at her lips. "Better than I have been in a while."

"Good." I ran my fingers through her dark hair but couldn't raise much of a smile.

She tilted her head. "You're tense." Her eyebrow arched. "Kind of like you were when you . . ."

I released my breath. "Just mentally debriefing, I guess."

"Mentally debriefing?" Her brow furrowed. "How so?"

"I . . ." I chewed my lip. "To be honest, I hadn't really thought about what it would be like to go there again. Being in bed with someone, I mean."

"I know the feeling. But . . . it was good, right? It wasn't—"

"Everything was perfect." I lifted my head and kissed her lightly. "The only problems were"—I tapped my temple—"in here."

Kim's lips tightened. "So it doesn't go away?"

"I don't know if it does or not. I really don't." I squeezed her hand. "I wish I could say it does, but . . ."

She nodded.

"It's totally different with you versus with them, but it's . . ."

"You're still vulnerable."

"Yeah." I brought her hand up and pressed my lips to the backs of her fingers. "Makes it hard to . . ." I laughed humorlessly. "Well, let's just say that was the longest dry spell I've ever had."

"Really?"

"Oh yeah. The first couple of years after I enlisted, I fucked any girl that moved within a hundred-mile radius of whatever base or port I was at. And in high school, I definitely got around. Guys *and* girls."

Kim propped herself up on her arm. "You're bi?"

"No. I was still figuring myself out back then." I paused, gazing up at the ceiling. "You know what's kind of weird?"

"Hmm?"

"I haven't been interested in men since I was seventeen, but ever since I was assaulted in Afghanistan"—I turned to her—"I've thought about it."

"What do you mean?"

"Maybe it would be different if I'd never been with a guy before. But ever since Afghanistan, it's hard for me to remember what it was like to be with a guy and not be afraid of him. And on some really weird level, I've wanted to spend a night with a man again just to put that to rest." I shook my head. "It sounds ridiculous, I know. I'm not attracted to guys, I just want to go back to thinking, *This isn't my thing, but it's not horrible*, you know?"

"I don't think it's ridiculous. Anything to clear out the poison."

"Yes, exactly."

She brushed a few strands of hair out of my face. "Well, this has helped me, too." She laughed softly, almost playfully. "And I'll bet money my dry spell was longer than yours."

"Oh yeah?"

"Yeah, it's been . . ." Her eyes lost focus for a few seconds. "Four years, I think?"

"No kidding?"

"Ironic, isn't it?" Her lips quirked. "Everyone thinks I'm a whore, but I've only been with three girls. And no guys. I mean, except—"

"No guys," I said. "If it wasn't consensual, it doesn't count."

"Thank fuck for that," she muttered. "But yeah, all I ever had was a couple of girlfriends when I was a teenager. Didn't really date much because I was too busy with school."

"Really?"

Kim nodded. "I was kind of obsessive about my grades."

I raised my eyebrows. "Were you?"

"Oh yeah. I wanted to join the Navy, and I didn't want to wind up in some shit job. So I was stacking the deck."

"I'm surprised you didn't go to the Academy."

She smiled shyly. "I wanted to be a cop."

"Funny." I laughed. "I always swore I'd never *date* a cop."

"Well, I said I'd never date another Sailor."

I smoothed her hair. "I don't see why we can't do this, though. We obviously click."

"We should probably keep it quiet at work."

"Definitely. Knowing the jackwagons running our command, they'd find a way to hem us up for fraternization." I rolled my eyes. "They tried to do that with a couple of second classes last year. They made one the 'supervisor' over the other, then tried to get them in trouble for fraternizing because they hung out on the weekends."

"Oh, I fucking *dare* Stanton to try to nail anyone for fraternization," Kim growled.

"Seriously."

She held my gaze. "And, uh, I swear, this wasn't what I had in mind when I pinged you on Skype."

"It wasn't what I had in mind when I came here." I caressed her face. "But it's definitely a silver lining."

"Yeah, it is."

I smoothed her hair. "And just so we're clear, I am so sorry for being a bitch when you first came to the command. I should've known better. God knows I know how hard it is to be yourself in this environment."

"It's okay." She shrugged. "The only thing you had to go by was what I showed you."

"Still. I shouldn't have . . ."

"It's done. Don't worry about it." She trailed her fingers up and down my arm. "The hardest part is I don't know which makes people think less of me: when I'm the cold bitch or when I'm the party girl." She met my eyes. "We can't win, you know?"

"No, we can't. And we have to do whatever it takes to protect ourselves."

"But how the hell are we supposed to know how to protect ourselves without it backfiring?"

"I wish I knew." Stroking her cheek, I added, "But at least we're both safe here tonight."

Her smile was slow to form, but it did materialize, and she moved closer to me. "This is the safest I've felt in a while, to be honest."

"Me too." I kissed her forehead. "We have to go back to that bullshit eventually, but . . ."

She raised her chin and brushed my lips with hers. "But not tonight."

"No." I wrapped my arms around her. "Not tonight."

CHAPTER 17

KIM

I couldn't remember the last time I'd woken up tangled in someone else's limbs, and I'd forgotten how much I loved it. As the daylight poked in between the burlap curtains, I didn't want to move. I was seriously tempted to just lie there all day, my skin touching Reese's, and not do a damned thing that required getting out of this bed.

But at a little past eight, the alarm on Reese's phone chirped. She grumbled something—I couldn't quite understand it, but knowing her it was probably obscene—and reached for the bedside table to shut off the noise.

I thought she'd roll over and go back to sleep. Who sets an alarm on vacation, anyway? But she sat up and stretched.

"Come back to bed," I murmured.

"I would." She leaned down and kissed my temple. "But I need to go for a run."

"We're on vacation."

"I know. Still . . ."

"Overachiever."

She laughed, kissed me again, and got out of bed. "I'll be back in a bit."

"I'll be here."

After she left, I debated going back to sleep, but I was already awake, so I sat up. Damn it, why were my muscles so stiff? I expected to be tired and achy after fooling around with Reese for most of the night, but this was different. This wasn't fatigue. Everything was tense. Knotted.

Oh.

Right.

Because this wasn't over yet.

Sighing, I kneaded my shoulder. Maybe a hot shower would help. Couldn't hurt, anyway.

In the shower, I flattened my palms against the cracked tile wall, closed my eyes, and let the hot water run over my neck and shoulders.

We're on vacation, I heard myself mumbling to Reese.

Except it wasn't a vacation. I hadn't come here to relax. I sure as fuck hadn't come here to have sex. I wasn't complaining about everything we'd done, of course. Things were great with Reese, and I hoped, hoped, hoped they could continue like that when we went back to Okinawa.

But whether they did or not, the rest of this situation would continue. I still had to make a report against Stanton. There'd be an investigation.

And I was still carrying his baby.

Until the day after tomorrow, anyway.

I shuddered, and though the water temperature hadn't changed, I was suddenly cold, so I shut off the shower and stepped out. As I dried myself, I avoided my fogged-up reflection in the tiny mirror.

T minus forty-eight hours, and I had to face the abortion clinic for the second time. What guarantee did I have that I wouldn't freak out again? I'd been on edge from the moment I'd walked in. Anything could've triggered that flashback. If it hadn't been the nurse encouraging me to lie back—

Just lie back. Relax.

—who was to say something else wouldn't have set me off?

Nausea rose in my throat. I leaned over the toilet, but after a few deep breaths, the sensation passed, so I stood upright and leaned on the door, the surface cool against my bare skin.

Chewing my lip, I looked down. I was still way too early to be showing, so the little "extra" above my belt was probably the result of stress eating or not spending as much time PTing as I should've. I doubted anyone else had noticed, considering how much I was "showing" on top. Goddamn. Another week or two and I'd need new bras. If people hadn't already noticed, they would soon.

Another week or two? Soon?

I let my head fall back against the door. No one would notice and I wouldn't have to buy bras or a maternity uniform because I wouldn't *be* pregnant after this week.

Would I?

I closed my eyes.

Just once, I needed something about this fucking debacle to be simple.

I was pulling on my sandals when Reese came back in.

"Hey. How was your run?"

"Would've been better if some lady's poodle hadn't tried to attack me, but otherwise . . ." She shrugged. Then she cocked her head. "Is something wrong?"

"Hmm? No. No. I'm . . ." I forced a smile. "Just not quite awake yet."

The creases in her forehead deepened, and I silently begged her to let it go.

Fortunately, she did. "I'm gonna grab a quick shower. Then, breakfast?"

The smile didn't take quite so much work this time. "Breakfast sounds like a winner."

"Good, because I'm starving."

"Hurry up and shower then, overachiever."

She playfully swatted my butt and then went in to take a shower. When she came back, I had just finished tying my damp hair into a ponytail.

As she dressed, I sat on the bed. "I, um . . . can we talk about something before we go out?"

Reese glanced up from zipping her shorts. "Sure. What's up?"

I set my shoulders back. "I'm canceling the abortion."

Her eyebrows jumped. "Are you?"

Cringing, I nodded. "I know I can't keep the baby. But I'm . . ." I glanced down and realized I'd put my hand over my still-mostly-flat belly. "I just don't feel right about this part."

"Oh thank God." She sat beside me. "I didn't want to talk you out of it, but . . ."

Eyeing her, I said, "But you didn't approve?"

"*Approve* is not the word I'd use." She tucked a strand of hair behind my ear. "But it never felt like this was what *you* wanted."

My shoulders sagged. "It wasn't. Isn't. The thing is, even though I know it's the . . . well, not the easiest, but the simplest way to cut ties with Stanton, I can't make myself believe I'm doing it because I want to. I agreed to it because I didn't see any other way. But it doesn't feel right to do it just because he wants it, you know?"

Reese nodded. "Absolutely."

"I know I can't raise this kid, and I don't want to be tied to Stanton for the rest of my life." I glanced down at the hand that I still had over my belly. "But I just can't do it."

"Then don't." She pulled me into a gentle embrace and kissed my forehead. "If it doesn't feel like the right thing, it probably isn't."

Our eyes met, and my heart jumped into my throat. "Shit."

"What?"

"What about our, uh, deal?" I swallowed. "You know what happened. And we agreed you'd report things, so he'll—"

"I know." She smoothed my hair. "But don't you dare go through with this just so I don't get in trouble. We'll figure something out, but . . . don't. Not unless it's what you want."

"It isn't."

"Then there's your answer."

"But what *do* we do? I told you what happened because I was going to get the abortion, but now we're in a bad spot."

Reese sighed. "I don't know. I really don't. But I promise you, I'm not going to run in and report this when we get back."

"Thank you," I whispered.

She smiled and kissed me gently. "Go ahead and make the call. I bet you'll feel better afterward."

"You're probably right." I found the appointment-confirmation card in my purse, picked up the motel's phone and dialed the number for the clinic.

When the receptionist answered, I said, "Hi. I'd like . . ." I glanced up at Reese, and she nodded. I moistened my lips. "I need to cancel an appointment."

"All right, ma'am. Can I get your name?"

"Kim Lockhoff." I spelled my last name for her, and as we went through the motions of canceling my procedure, my stomach fluttered, but for once, I didn't feel like I was going to be sick. As I hung up the phone, something in my chest settled. This whole thing was far from over, but I felt better. I finally felt like I had *some* say about my own future.

I blew out a breath and met Reese's eyes. "Okay. It's done."

She sat beside me again and hugged me. "Good. I'm proud of you. It takes some balls not to let that asshole bully you into something like this."

Sighing, I rested my head against her. "Just wish I could've sprouted those balls when I was in his office."

"Honey, you were protecting yourself." She kissed the top of my head. "That wasn't being weak, it was keeping a bad situation from getting worse."

I shuddered. "I guess it could've been worse, couldn't it?"

"Yeah. It could've." She lifted my chin and kissed my lips this time. "And I'm really, really glad it didn't turn out that way."

"Me too."

We held on to each other for a long moment before she drew back and met my eyes. "You know, since our leave was extended, we still have a few days left in Hawaii."

I scowled. "Doesn't seem long enough. Ugh. I just . . . do not want to go back."

"In your shoes, I wouldn't, either. But for the time being, you're on vacation. Might as well enjoy it."

"True." I hesitated. "You really think that's, uh, ethical, though? Considering why we're here?"

Reese raised her eyebrows. "Do you really think Stanton is going to try and fuck with you over how you spend your time on Oahu?"

I hesitated but then smiled. "Yeah, good point."

"Exactly. So we're going to go out and have a good time, and he can suck it." She put her hand on my leg. "So, where do you want to go?"

I thought for a moment. "Well, Diamond Head is probably out today, but we could check out the USS Arizona Memorial."

"Oh, good idea." She held up the car keys. "You driving, or am I?"

"You drive."

"On it. Let's go."

Hand in hand, we headed out to explore the rest of Oahu.

CHAPTER 18

REESE

We landed on Okinawa twenty-four hours before our leave chits expired. I took Kim straight to the acute care clinic on Camp Courtney to get a light duty chit and to have her pregnancy noted in her medical record.

I went into the exam room with her, and we played silently on our phones until the corpsman came in.

"I'm HM1 Davis." She shook our hands. Then she opened Kim's chart. "And just to verify, your pregnancy test did come back positive."

Kim closed her eyes and exhaled. I hadn't realized how much her shoulders had bunched up until then, as they slowly relaxed.

"You okay?" HM1 Davis asked.

"Yeah." Kim opened her eyes. "Isn't like it's a surprise."

The corpsman arched an eyebrow. "Well, I have some information for you." She handed over a stack of pamphlets and paperwork. "You'll want to get registered with the hospital on Camp Lester as soon as you can, and they can get you into some of the childbirth classes."

Kim blinked. "Okay."

The corpsman continued through various recommendations—a schedule of appointments with one of the base OBs, symptoms to watch out for, a regimen of prenatal vitamins. Kim nodded as Davis spoke but didn't say anything. I couldn't imagine what was going through her mind. All that bullshit overwhelmed me and I wasn't the one who had to deal with it.

"Now—" the corpsman hesitated, but then held up one of the pamphlets "—pregnant women are at a much higher risk for domestic violence. This has a list of numbers you can—"

"I'm an MA," Kim said with a dry, halfhearted laugh. "I know who I can contact."

"Okay, good. There are some other numbers on here, though. We recommend all patients take them, even if they don't think they're necessary."

Kim glanced at me. Without a word, she took the pamphlet and added it to the stack of paperwork beside her on the exam table.

The corpsman scanned her chart, then set it aside. "Do you have any questions or concerns at this point?"

Kim shook her head. The corpsman jotted a few more notes and then released her.

After Kim had signed out, we headed for the parking lot. Once we were outside, Kim leaned against my car while I lit a cigarette.

I took a few drags, letting the nicotine get into my system. As I tapped the ashes over the pavement, I said, "How are you holding up?"

"I still think I made the right decision."

"Then you did." I hugged her with one arm, carefully keeping my cigarette away from her. "I know there aren't any easy options right now, but I think you've done the best you can."

"I've tried, anyway."

I let her go and stepped back to take another drag. "Out of curiosity, I . . . Well, when the corpsman said your test was positive, you looked kind of, I don't know—"

"Relieved?"

"Yeah."

She shrugged. "I don't know. I guess I needed someone tell me this is really happening. Everything's been so up in the air lately, at least something was in black-and-white, you know?"

"Huh. I hadn't thought of it that way, but it makes sense."

"As much sense as anything in this situation can make." She blew out a breath. "I guess I should give my light duty chit to Gutiérrez."

"You're still on leave until tomorrow."

"Yeah, but I might as well get it over with." She shivered in spite of the tropical heat. "How long do you think it'll take till Stanton finds out?"

"Depends." I squeezed her hand. "Do you want to let him find out? Or tell him?"

"I don't even want to look at him." She shuddered.

"I don't blame you."

Kim shifted her weight. "Then again, if I tell him to his face, at least I get to be the one in control."

"Good point. Assuming he doesn't try to put a hand on you." I tightened my grasp. "If he does, I swear to God—"

"Threatening me into getting an abortion is one thing." She met my eyes as she ran her thumb along my finger. "Getting violent and possibly causing me to miscarry? I don't think even Stanton is that stupid."

"Let's hope."

"Yeah. But . . . Ugh. I can't deal with him. Not right this second. I think I'll start with Gutiérrez."

"Do you want me to come with you?"

Her eyes widened. "Will you?"

"Of course. When do you want to go?"

"The sooner the better."

I glanced at my watch. "He's probably in the office right now."

"Let's go."

Alejandro's office door was open as usual, and MA1 Harris wasn't around.

"MA1?" I said. "You busy?"

He looked up from a logbook. "Oh. I didn't expect you back until tomorrow." He glanced past me. "Either of you."

"We're still on leave." I gestured for Kim to follow me, and she shut the door behind us. "But MA3 needed to speak to you."

"Oh. Uh, okay."

Kim cleared her throat and handed him a folded piece of paper. "I need to go on light duty."

"Light duty?" His features tightened with confusion, and then he looked at the chit he'd taken from her. His lips parted. His eyes flicked toward me, then to Kim, eyebrows rising. "Is this . . ." He glanced at me again.

Shoulders pushed back, Kim shifted her weight. "Until I have the baby. And then, of course, I'll need to take some maternity leave."

He pressed his lips together, and maybe he couldn't quite hide it, or maybe I just knew him too well, but I saw the *Oh, shit . . .* flickering across his face, plain as day. He quickly schooled his expression, though. "All right. Uh, it looks like you'll be on dispatch for a while."

Kim grimaced. "That's the only thing available?"

"Yeah. Most of admin's overstaffed right now." He shrugged. "Dispatch is all I've got."

Her shoulders fell. "There isn't anything over on Kadena? Like in Pass & ID or something?"

Alejandro studied her, a million questions written in his creased brow. "I'd, uh, have to call and find out, but they haven't been asking for bodies, so . . ."

Kim glanced at me. So did Alejandro.

I chewed my lip. "MA3, would you mind excusing us for a minute?"

They both tensed, but Alejandro said nothing, and Kim quickly slipped out of the office.

When the door closed behind her, I faced him. "Would I be out of line asking you to get her into Pass & ID as a personal favor?"

"A personal—" Alejandro put up his hands. "Okay, can we back up a second here? I mean, what exactly is going on? I thought she went to Hawaii so she could get—"

"Did she tell you that?"

His mouth opened, but he quickly closed it, and his posture stiffened.

I folded my arms. "Or did *he* tell you?"

Alejandro swallowed. "It doesn't take much to put two and two together."

"Then I don't need to spell it out, do I?"

"Uh, no." He glanced at the door. "But she just told me she's having the baby."

I nodded.

He pinched the bridge of his nose. "Jesus Christ." Dropping his hand, he added, "She's playing with fire, Reese."

"Actually, she's playing with a very shitty hand and doing the best she can with it."

"What did she think was going to happen when she—" He shook his head. "Seriously, is she surprised this happened?"

I swallowed the bile rising in my throat, reminding myself over and over that he didn't know the whole story. "Somehow I don't think Stanton thought it all the way through, either, but—"

"I'm not saying he was any less of an idiot, but the fact is her involvement is a lot harder to hide than his. Any idiot would know that sleeping with a higher-up like that would make the—"

"For God's sake," I hissed. "Who do you really think was in control of that situation?"

"She's an adult," he snapped. "If I have to string up all the other idiots who do stupid things while they're drunk, I can't be bending over backward for her for doing the same fucking thing."

I ground my teeth. I was already dangerously close to tipping my hand. "Would it really be that much of a hassle for you? To get her out of this precinct for a little while?"

"There's only so much I can do and you know it."

"I think you have more options than you're letting on. My question is how worried are you that those options would affect your chances of making chief?"

He narrowed his eyes. "You're out of line, MA2."

I bristled. "Sorry, *MA1*."

We glared at each other.

He folded his arms across his camo blouse. "You know, a week or two ago, you were pissed at me for even asking you to make sure she was all right. Now you want me to jump through hoops to keep her away from the father of her kid. What the fuck is—"

"What I want is for you to step up and help one of your Sailors. If you can find time in between kissing Lieutenant Stanton's ass."

He blinked, and my teeth snapped shut. Friend or not, he *was* still my LPO.

"You know me," he growled. "And you know damn well this isn't about kissing anyone's ass."

"Isn't it? Because it seems to me you've gotten pretty friendly with Stanton recently."

He rolled his eyes and exhaled sharply. "I'm friendly with Chief and Senior Chief, too, and I don't like them any more than I like him."

"So it's all political games."

"You know how this shit works."

"Yeah, I do. So is that the only reason you'll dig your heels in when it comes to protecting one of your Sailors?"

"Protecting?" He threw up his hands. "From *what*? It isn't like she's the one who has to go home and face the spouse she cheated on." He gestured in the general direction of Stanton's office. "He's got a hell of a lot more to lose than she does."

"Then maybe he should've thought of that, shouldn't he?"

"Isn't like he can do anything about it now." He waved sharply at the door. "Especially since she's apparently taken it upon herself to not do anything."

My mouth fell open. "You really think she should have gone through with it? Just so he didn't have to face his wife or—"

"No, that is not what I'm saying," he snarled. "I'm saying *she's* the one in control here, not him. So I'm hard-pressed to handle her with kid gloves." He stabbed a finger at me. "And you of all people know exactly why because you wanted nothing to do with this whole situation. What the fuck has changed?"

"I was wrong," I whispered. "About her."

He studied me. Then one eyebrow climbed his forehead. "How wrong? You went from not being able to look at her, to dashing off to Hawaii to be with her, to . . ." He pushed out a breath. "Please tell me you and she aren't—"

"That's none of your fucking business." I regretted the words before they were even out. I might as well have scrawled *Guilty as charged* across my forehead.

His other eyebrow rose, and his lips tightened. "So tell me how this conversation isn't a conflict of interest."

"Is it any more of one than you and Chief patting Stanton on the back for dodging a bullet so his wife didn't find out about what happened?"

Alejandro jumped so hard I thought he was going to fall backward.

"Yes, I overheard you." I curled my lip in disgust.

His expression hardened. "Don't act like you're a saint here. It wasn't very long ago you'd have been standing right there with me, and you probably would've had some choice words about her behavior."

"You're right. I would have." I raised my chin and glared back at him. "But I was wrong. Very, very wrong. And right now, she needs help from the few people she can trust in her chain of command, which pretty much boils down to you and me."

He watched me silently for a moment. "Is there something more to this story?"

I opened my mouth to reply, but stopped before I said anything Kim and I would both regret. "No. Just . . . a really shitty situation and two people who really don't need to be tripping over each other every day at work."

Alejandro shook his head. "Look, I don't envy her for the situation she's in, but she's a grown-ass adult who made a decision. If they're in a shitty situation or things are awkward between them, I can only do so much. I'm not a goddamned babysitter."

I bit back some blistering insubordination and lowered my voice. "Will you at least call Pass & ID and see if she can work there for a while?"

"I'll call them." He shrugged. "I can't make any promises."

"Thank you." I paused. "MA1."

His eyebrows flicked up, and then he set his jaw. "Dismissed, MA2."

I barely kept myself from slamming his office door behind me.

CHAPTER 19
KIM

Reese stepped out of Gutiérrez's office, and I took a step back.

"What . . . what happened? You look like you're ready to hit someone."

She took a deep breath and released slowly. "I need a cigarette."

I followed her out of the precinct and up to the smoke pit.

"So, what did he say?" I asked.

She lit her cigarette and pocketed the lighter. "Well, he's looking into Pass & ID."

"Awesome. Thank you."

She brought the cigarette back up to her lips. "I don't know how hard he's going to look, to be honest."

"Damn it."

"There isn't much he can do." She glanced at me through the thin cloud of smoke. "God knows whose side he's on these days, but I do know that without a formal complaint, he'll be hard-pressed to justify separating the two of you."

Sighing, I nodded. "I know."

"And even if you go over to Kadena to work in Pass & ID, you'll still technically be working for Stanton."

"Fine." I waved a hand. "I just can't be in the same building with him every day."

"I know." She took a long drag and blew out the smoke. "I don't even like being on the same island with him."

"Tell me about it. And I . . . Fuck, I need to talk to him." I stood a little straighter and steeled myself. "So he knows I didn't get the abortion."

Reese chewed her lip. "Are you sure?"

I nodded. "Better he hears it from me sooner than later. In fact, I'm going to do that now before my light duty chit gets to his desk." I turned to go.

"Kim." She stopped me with a hand on my arm. "You shouldn't face him on your own."

Eyes locked on hers, I gently freed my elbow. "I need to. I need him to know I'm not afraid of him."

"*Are* you afraid of him?"

I moistened my lips. "Of course I am." The hairs on the back of my neck stood on end. "But I don't want him to know that."

"Are you sure about this?"

"Yeah." *I think.* "There isn't much he can do in the office. Not with so many people around."

"True. But still . . ."

"I'll be okay." I took a step toward the precinct but glanced back. "Will you be here?"

"Of course." She dropped her cigarette and crushed it under her sneaker. "I'll wait for you in dispatch, so I'll be right down the hall."

"Okay. Thanks."

Back inside, I steeled myself and headed toward Stanton's office. His door was closed as always, so I knocked.

"Come in."

I took a deep breath—*I can do this*—and pushed open the door.

"MA3." He sat back in his chair. "I wasn't expecting to see you until tomorrow."

"My flight came in this morning, Sir."

He looked me up and down. "And how are you feeling?"

"I'll be fine, Sir." I reached into my pocket and withdrew the wrinkled envelope of cash. "I just came to give this back to you."

He eyed it but didn't reach for it. "What is that?"

"The money." I set it on his desk. "I'm returning it." The clinic had charged me for the cancellation, but I'd been able to scrounge up enough to cover the difference so I could pay every dime back to Stanton. No way in hell was I going to be in debt to a son of a bitch like him.

He picked up the envelope and lifted the flap enough to see the cash inside. Then his eyes flicked up to meet mine. "You had medical do it, then."

"No." I stood straighter, setting my jaw. "I canceled it, Sir."

His lips pulled into a thin line, and he rose. "What do you mean, you canceled it?"

"I mean, I canceled it. I'm not having it done." I swallowed. "Sir."

He came around the desk, every step slow and calculated. I refused to budge. No way in hell.

He stopped in front of me and folded his arms. "So if you weren't taking care of this *situation*, then what the fuck were you doing while you were on leave?"

"I'm not sure how that's any of your—"

"I signed an emergency leave chit for MA2 Marion to fly out there to be with you. Not so the two of you could fuck around in Hawaii."

I forced myself to hold his gaze. "I went to the clinic but then decided I couldn't go through with it."

He laughed humorlessly. "You decided you couldn't go through with it."

"Yes, Sir."

The laughter vanished, and the sudden fury in his eyes made my stomach clench. "You're a fucking idiot, MA3."

"Why?" My voice shook. "I'm not the one who fucked an unwilling woman. Without a condom, no less."

His features hardened even more, and suddenly I wished I had brought Reese in here. He wouldn't be stupid enough to get violent, would he? If he did, every MA within earshot would be here in seconds. Wouldn't they?

Because the man who'd forced me to have sex with him was certainly rational enough not to get violent when cornered.

Pregnant women are at a much higher risk for domestic violence.

Oh fuck.

I gulped.

His lips pulled into a bleached line. "Let's get one thing straight, right here, right now. No one in this command is going to believe for a second that I raped you. And you know damn well I *didn't*."

"Do I?"

His eyebrows rose. "You seem to be forgetting you're speaking to a superior officer, MA3."

"A married superior officer who had sex with a petty officer third class under his command?" My heart dropped as I realized I'd said it out loud.

"I would suggest you watch your step, MA3." He leaned in just enough to make me draw back. "Because there is a hell of a lot more on the line here than you think."

"Like what?"

"I believe you mean, like what, *Sir?*"

I swallowed. "Like what, Sir?"

"Your career, for one."

In spite of my pounding heart and shaking legs, I managed to snarl, "And yours, *Sir.*"

"Yes. And mine." He raised his hand, and I flinched, but he didn't hit me. Instead, he put his hand against the door beside my head, and now he was looming over me, so close I could almost feel his breath on my skin. *Again.*

"You should be aware," he growled, almost whispering, "that I will fight tooth and nail to keep you from damaging my career, my reputation, and my marriage. And no one is going to believe a notorious whore with only one chevron on her shoulder over me." He leaned in even closer, until our faces were nearly touching and I couldn't draw back any farther because of the door behind me. "Am I clear, MA3?"

I refused to break eye contact. "Yes, Sir."

"Good." He stepped back.

Oh thank God. I could breathe again. I flattened my palms against the door, leaning hard against it so my knees wouldn't shake out from under me.

Stanton was quiet but only for a moment. "Whatever you choose to do, mark my words. If it goes on record that this kid is mine, I will make *sure* you regret it." He snatched the envelope off the desk and shoved it toward me. "I'd suggest you get it done."

I took the envelope, glanced down at it, then up at him. "Noted, Sir."

And then I got the fuck out of there before I lost what little nerve I had left.

Outside, I shoved the envelope into my pocket, leaned against the wall, and waited for my heartbeat to slow down.

So much for not letting him intimidate me.

"Kim?" Reese's voice turned my head. "Are you okay?"

I pushed myself off the wall and started toward her. She looked me up and down and quickly herded me into an empty conference room.

I sank into a folding chair, rubbing my temples. Chair legs scraped on the floor, and Reese sat down beside me.

She rubbed the back of my neck. "What happened?"

"It went about as well as I expected."

"Shit. That bad?"

"Are you surprised?"

"Well . . . no."

I sat back and met her eyes. "I really need to get out of this office. I don't care if Gutiérrez sends me over to Kadena or if he has me checking IDs at the gate. I just . . ." I shook my head. "I can't deal with him."

"I know." She took my hand and squeezed it. "And reporting him—"

Almost instantaneously, my eyes teared up.

"Oh, sweetheart." She wrapped her arms around me. "He threatened you again, didn't he?"

"Of course he did." I sniffed and held onto her. "Same threat as before. That I'll regret it if anyone finds out this is his kid, and he'll . . . Fuck, I don't know what to do."

"I know. Fuck that son of a bitch." She kissed the top of my head and sighed into my hair. "I'm so sorry, Kim."

After a moment, I sat up and wiped my eyes. "I guess, well . . . The thing is, I don't have a choice. I can't go through with an abortion. He's got me backed into a corner about pressing charges. There's really only one thing I *can* do."

"What's that?"

I moistened my lips. "Have the baby. Give it up for adoption. And move on with my life." I held her gaze, silently begging her not to remind me that she was obligated to report Stanton on my behalf. I had a choice. Legally, she didn't.

But she just nodded and took my hand. "Okay. Whatever happens, I'll be there."

I brought her hand up and kissed her fingers. "Thank you."

"Don't mention it," she whispered and hugged me again. "Now let's get the fuck out of this place."

"Good idea."

CHAPTER 20
REESE

Two cigarettes after we'd left the precinct, Kim and I made our way to my car.

As I waited for the AC to cool everything off, I turned to her. "We're both back to work tomorrow. I guess I should take you home so we can get unpacked."

"Oh God." Kim pinched the bridge of her nose. "Goddamn it. I don't want to go back there."

"Back where? The barracks?"

She nodded.

"What? Why?"

"Word was getting around. Even before I went on leave." She lowered her hand and leaned over, hugging herself. "I heard some of the guys in the barracks talking about how hot pregnant women are. And fucking them is awesome because you don't have to use a rubber."

"Yeah, guys talk."

She eyed me. "And they've conveniently brought up that subject three times while I was within earshot."

"Fuck . . ."

"Yeah. And . . ." She swallowed, and her jaw tightened as she stared out the window.

"What? Tell me?"

"They, um . . ." She pulled in a deep breath as she turned to me. "I heard someone say if a chick's pregnant, she obviously, well, wants it. To be fucked, I mean."

"Jesus."

She sniffed. "Isn't it nice that our chain of command leads by example?"

I couldn't even muster a smile. I reached across the console and held her hand in her lap. "Sweetheart, do you feel safe in the barracks?"

Kim shuddered.

"Why don't you come stay with me?"

She turned her head. "I'm an E4. I can't live off-base."

"Under the circumstances, I don't think you should live *on*-base." I squeezed her hand. "It's up to you."

"You really don't mind?"

"Not in the least."

"Okay. Thanks."

I took her back to the barracks so we could pick up a few things for her. As she packed, I glanced down the hall. A few doors were open and male voices talked shit over video games while a couple of guys in uniform headed out, probably on their way to work. Only a door and thin walls separated her from any of them. I could only imagine how she felt living here. If it was anything like how I'd felt after Afghanistan, then she needed to get the hell out of here and go someplace safe. Maybe she couldn't get away from these guys at work, but she could at least undress, shower, and sleep without being terrified every time she heard someone walk past her door.

After she'd packed, I took her seabag and hoisted it onto my shoulders. She slid her laptop and a paperback that had been sitting by her bed into a small backpack.

She followed me to my apartment, which was about fifteen minutes from White Beach, and we carried everything upstairs.

I set her seabag beside the couch in the living room. "It's not much, but you can stay as long as you need to."

"Thanks. I really appreciate it." She set on the edge of a couch cushion. "I feel a lot better being away from that place, at least for now."

"I don't blame you." I sat beside her and put my hand on her knee. "And I have to admit, I kind of like having you here anyway."

"Yeah?" She finally smiled. "Why's that?"

I wrapped my arms around her. "Why do you think?"

She let herself be pulled closer, and when she released her breath, the knots in her shoulders seemed to vanish all at once.

"I like being here. Being with you is so much safer." She lifted her chin and kissed me gently. "But that's definitely not the only reason I like being with you."

"I would hope not." I leaned in and pressed my lips to hers.

And didn't pull back.

I'd only meant for a light, affectionate kiss, but the softness of her mouth was addictive. And after the day we'd had, all the bullshit and stress and fucking chaos, I couldn't resist the reprieve that her warm embrace offered. One kiss, a tighter embrace, and the next thing I knew, we were way too close for this to end anytime soon.

I broke the kiss and murmured, "I've, um . . . I haven't shown you the bedroom."

"Hmm, no, you haven't."

"I should fix that." I took her hand, and she let me lead her down the short hallway.

As I was pulling her back into my arms, she scanned our surroundings, and a smirk played at her lips. "These walls concrete? Like in the barracks?"

"Yep." I snaked my hands around her waist. "Which means the neighbors won't hear a thing."

She giggled and pulled me closer. "That's what they think."

"Mmm, why do I get the feeling you see this as a challenge?"

She nudged me toward the bed. "And you don't?"

"I never said that." I dragged her down onto the bed with me, and the second my back hit the mattress, we were too busy kissing to bother with playful banter. Too busy kissing and too busy getting past all these clothes to the skin underneath.

We quickly stripped off everything from the waist up. My bra hadn't even hit the floor before Kim moved in and started on my breasts. She spent ages on one nipple, teasing with lips, tongue, and teeth, before moving to the other.

I slid a hand beneath her shirt and found her breast. Her nipple was rock hard, and when my fingertip brushed it, she jumped.

"Still sensitive?"

"Mm-hmm. But keep . . . keep . . ."

"Don't mind if I do." I pinched her nipple gently, but firmly, and kissed my way down the side of her neck. Moaning, she squirmed under me, pressing her breasts into my hands and her body against mine.

"We should really do something about all these clothes," I said.

"Mm-hmm. But I like . . . what you're . . ."

I pinched her nipple a little harder, and she groaned.

"*Fuck*, Reese."

"We should get undressed," I whispered. "So I can touch you all over."

"Yes. *Now.*"

We separated, and she grabbed my waistband. Her hands were steadier than mine, and she managed to get the button and zipper undone with less trouble than I probably would've had. Then she pushed my shorts over my hips, and I sighed as her warm hands slid over my newly bared skin. In between kissing and touching, we shed the rest of our clothes and pulled each other close on top of my comforter.

She ground against me. "Fuck. I can't get enough of you."

"Me neither." I kissed her. "So you didn't get bored with this in Hawaii?"

She laughed. "Oh fuck no. Did you?"

"Not even a little." I traced her sides with my palms. "I wanted to stay another month just so we could do more."

She moaned. "We can do everything here."

"Mm-hmm."

"Can we just stay here all night?"

"If we do," I murmured, "we're not going to be able to move tomorrow."

"I don't want to move tomorrow." She curved her hand around the back of my neck. "I just want you."

"Oh God . . ." My nipples grazed hers, sending a tremor through me. "The feeling's mutual, baby."

"Thought so," she said and kissed me.

Hands all over skin, breasts against breasts, lips and tongues playing—God, I really didn't give a fuck if I could move tomorrow, either, as long as this didn't stop anytime soon. And she was going to be staying here? In my apartment? In my bed? Jesus . . .

Kim pushed me onto my back and parted my legs. As she sat up and straddled my thigh, drawing my other leg up toward her hip, my breath caught.

Oh yes.

Yes, please . . .

She slid forward, and I exhaled as her pussy pushed up against mine. Then her hips were in motion, and holy fuck, I loved the way she felt, the way she rubbed over my clit. I met her rhythm, rocking my hips with hers so we rubbed together just right.

I couldn't get enough of running my hands all over her naked skin. Of having her against me and above me as she brought me closer and closer to what promised to be an *intense* orgasm.

And the way she moved her hips was fucking *divine.*

"Jesus, Kim." I licked my lips. "You feel amazing."

She grinned. "So do you."

Her breasts bounced in time with her thrusts, and I couldn't resist cupping them. As I teased her nipples again, she closed her eyes and exhaled, her rhythm faltering for a second before she recovered and ground even harder. Not hard enough to be painful, but teetering right there on that fine line between perfect and too much.

"Oh fuck, baby." I swept my tongue across my lips. "I'm so . . . I am so gonna come if you . . ."

She whimpered softly. "Me too. Fuck . . ."

I closed my eyes and moaned. I was so fucking close, my whole body trembling as cool electricity surged through my veins. So close. So, so close. Right on the edge. Nothing existed but that point of delicious contact, where her pussy rubbed against mine and sent me higher and higher and higher until—

"Oh fuck!" My eyes flew open, and my back arched off the bed. "Fuck . . ." She didn't stop, and neither did my orgasm, and I was sure I was going to black out or fall to pieces or . . . or *something.* I let go of a loud cry, and the neighbors probably heard me, but I didn't care.

Kim moaned. Her rhythm fell apart. Then she did. She dug her fingers into my leg, pulling it harder against her hip as if she just needed something to hold on to, and she threw her head back as her whole body trembled above mine.

We both relaxed. She let my leg slide down, and I drew her down on top of me. Closing my eyes, I stroked her hair, and we just lay there for the longest time, wrapped up in each other while we caught our breath. I was distantly aware of the shitstorm still going on in our professional world, but here in this one, everything was perfect. Warm skin against warm skin, both of us breathing in unison as our hearts slowly came down. It just didn't get any better than this.

I had nearly dozed off when Kim murmured, "What's that sound?"

"That— Shit! That's my phone."

She lifted herself off me, and I grabbed it from the nightstand.

I didn't even need to look at the caller ID. The ringtone said it all.

"MA2 Marion."

"Hey, it's Alejan— It's MA1."

I winced. "Hey."

He cleared his throat. "I pulled some strings. I left a message for Lockhoff, but figured . . . I figured you might see her. If you do, would you tell her she starts at Pass & ID tomorrow morning at 0800? Please?"

Kim didn't answer to me, so this was definitely outside of protocol, but I knew Alejandro. This was *I want you to know I did what I could* wrapped up in professionalism.

I wrapped my arm around Kim's shoulders and kissed her forehead. "Thanks. I'll pass the message along."

CHAPTER 21
KIM

"**H**ere's your new ID." I slid the warm laminated card under the window at my Pass & ID station. "Is there anything else I can do for you?"

"No, thank you." The woman—an Air Force wife who'd misplaced her ID—smiled, then got up and left, and I called out the next number in the queue.

After a week, I pretty much knew the routine. Working in Pass & ID was boring and repetitive, but at least it kept me away from Stanton. His office was back at the precinct on White Beach, while I was a good forty-five minutes away behind a desk on Kadena Air Base.

That in itself pissed me off. He'd raped me. He'd made this whole thing happen. He was the one who'd done something wrong, but I was the one who had to be pulled off the streets and stuck in the Navy's version of the DMV.

Of course, it had been somewhat inevitable. I was pregnant. Light duty was part of the game. And, hell, I'd take any physical distance I could get from Stanton.

The clerk beside me called out, "Number thirty-six."

While I processed yet another dependent who'd lost her ID card, I glanced past her at the people waiting. A woman sitting at the end of a row of chairs looked at her number. Then she leaned over to another woman and held up her ticket. As I watched, they traded numbers.

"Number thirty-seven, please."

The other woman got up and headed over to the window. That was . . . weird.

As the other clerks and I continued to process people, the woman continued swapping her ticket with people sitting around her. What the hell? Was she really that hard up for daytime entertainment that she needed to wait an extra forty minutes just so she could watch the end of *Maury* on the communal television?

I finished processing the lost ID card, and after that person had gone, I called out, "Number forty-one, please."

The woman who'd been trading numbers with everyone stood and made her way to the chair in front of my window.

My chest tightened. What the hell was going on? I didn't recognize her, so I didn't think she was someone coming back to have me fix something I'd screwed up.

She sat down and folded her hands on top of the Coach bag in her lap.

I gulped. "How may I help you?"

"You're MA3 Lockhoff, yes?"

As if she couldn't read my name tape and the chevrons on my collar, but I nodded anyway.

She sat up straighter, her cheeks tensing as she clenched her teeth. "I need to talk to you."

"Um, okay?"

She looked me right in the eye. "My name is Susan Stanton."

My stomach flipped. I should've known she was an officer's wife. They had a certain air about them that the enlisted wives didn't usually have.

"Um. I see." I swallowed. "What can I do for you, Mrs. Stanton?"

"I'm assuming you're familiar with my husband."

A bit too familiar. "Yes."

"And you may or may not know he has two years left before he retires."

And thank God for that.

"Uh . . ."

She set her jaw. "I understand you're considering filing . . ." She glanced back and forth, then lowered her voice. "That you're considering filing 'charges' against him."

He'd fessed up to the wife? That was surprising.

"Well, if you know about that, then you know what happened."

She laughed humorlessly. "I know that an entitled little whore slept with my husband."

Of course you do. "And that she's having his baby?"

Susan stiffened, and through taut lips, she muttered, "Yes. I'm aware of that."

"Then I don't know what you want me to say."

"I want you to tell me why on earth you want the whole world to believe he *raped* you."

I held her gaze. "Because he did."

Her head tilted just so, her eyes narrowed. It was probably the look she gave her kids when they were feeding her bullshit. I felt like a prisoner visited by someone on the outside, listening to the well-dressed lady tell me how my choices and actions were affecting everyone else. How I was hurting people and making their lives hell and had no one to blame but myself while I sat here behind the glass in my uniform.

"Do you want the whole story?" I kept my voice low. "Because I'm pretty sure he didn't give you all the details."

"No, I do not," she growled. "But you are going to ruin our family's life."

"What about *my* life?" I snapped back.

She sighed heavily and did that impatient head-tilt again. "Listen, sweetheart. You made a mistake. Plenty of girls in the military do the same thing. But one time doesn't make you a tramp. People will forget." Her eyes narrowed. "But they won't forget when you accuse someone of being a rapist just to cover your own tracks."

My mouth fell open. "What? You think I'm just doing this so people don't think I'm a slut?"

Her lips tightened, and one pencil-thin eyebrow arched. "I think that ship has already sailed."

"Then why would I bother making up—"

"I don't know, and I don't care." She leaned closer to the window. "But I would suggest you reconsider."

"Your husband has already suggested that. Did you know he threatened me?"

She laughed dryly. "Oh, darling. Aren't you familiar with the saying 'Hell hath no fury like a woman scorned'?"

I clenched my teeth. God knew what Stanton had told her. In his mind, I'd probably dragged *him* from the party and seduced him.

"Listen." She folded her hands on the desk and leaned in even closer. "I know my husband is sometimes unfaithful. I don't like it, and I'd do anything to stop it. But he is *not* a rapist."

"How do you know?" I asked through my teeth, struggling to keep my voice down. "You weren't there."

"I know my husband."

"And I know *myself,* damn it!" I smacked my palm on the desk, and all the chatter around us instantly stopped. Everyone stared.

Susan's eyes flicked back and forth. My face burned.

She sat up straighter and gathered her Coach bag. "You think about what I've said. I assure you, you are making a huge mistake even thinking about filing charges against him."

She didn't wait for a response. She stood, shouldered the bag, and stalked out of the building.

I sat back, releasing my breath.

My supervisor touched my shoulder. "You okay, MA2?"

"I'm . . ." *Oh, Christ, don't cry. Not here.* "Do you mind if I step out for a minute?"

"Yeah, sure." He gestured at the door Susan Stanton had just gone through. "What was that all about, anyway?"

"Nothing." I waved a hand as I stood. "Just some . . . some personal bullshit."

"You're pretty rattled, though."

I quickly wiped my eyes. "It's okay. Just hormones." God, I hated hiding behind that, but all I could do was play the cards I'd been dealt.

"Oh. Right." He cleared his throat. "Take your time."

"Thanks."

I went into the half-filled storage room we used as a break room and dropped into a chair. I rubbed my temples, breathing slowly and evenly to ward off any nausea that might decide to join this party as I replayed my conversation with Mrs. Stanton.

Anger burned hotter in my chest than it had since the night her asshole husband had raped me. I'd been furious when Reese had all but rolled her eyes at the suggestion that I'd been assaulted, but she'd apologized repeatedly, especially after she'd heard the whole story.

But this?

This was bullshit.

The woman who lived with him, who'd been married to him for years and years, the mother of his children—*she* was threatening me now? Taking her husband at his word, even though she knew damn well he cheated on her sometimes.

I sat up. Something cold replaced the anger.

He'd cheated before. More than once.

But was I the only . . .

Oh God.

What if I *wasn't* the only one? More to the point, what were the odds he'd had consensual affairs all these years and then randomly decided he'd fuck me whether I liked it or not?

And if I let this one go, how many more would come after me?

I pulled my phone out of my pocket and sent Reese a text.

Can you meet me at White Beach?

CHAPTER 22

REESE

need to go back to White Beach."

"Again?" Weiss groaned. "What does Gutiérrez want this time?"

I swallowed. "I don't know. Sorry."

To Kim, I wrote back, *I'm on my way there now.*

"How long you think this is going to take?" Weiss asked.

"Don't know. Why don't you wait for me over at the E-Club, and I'll text you when we're done."

"Eh. Sounds good. I was getting hungry anyway."

I forced a laugh. "You're always hungry."

"And your ass is always getting called back to White Beach midshift, so I think we're even."

"Works for me."

My phone buzzed.

I'm not off shift yet. Be there ASAP.

My stomach twisted and churned. Whatever it was, she wanted to discuss it in person. No point asking her to elaborate via text.

Weiss dropped me off in front of the precinct. I debated having a cigarette, but I'd already had half a pack today, mostly after we'd responded to a domestic call this morning. Whatever Kim needed would probably warrant the rest of the pack—might as well wait.

Inside, I found four of the guys chilling behind the desk, waiting for shift change.

"Hey, MA2," Barkley said.

"Hey." I took off my cover and gestured at the door. "When MA3 Lockhoff gets here, could you send her back to dispatch?" Seemed like as good a place as any to hang out while I waited, and Stanton didn't usually show his face at that end of the hall. Better than sitting up here with these clowns.

"Sure thing."

"Thanks."

I stepped out into the hall and was about to head back to dispatch, but—

"Man, have you seen Lockhoff since she got back off leave?" Lee laughed. "God*damn*."

"Yeah!" Barkley chuckled. "The Titty Fairy has arrived."

This shit again?

All of them burst out laughing. My heart sank, and I backtracked, listening as they went on.

"I'm telling you, now's a good time to tap that. No rubber or nothing."

"Dude, you're insane. I told you before, that girl's been *around*."

"I'll bet her crabs have herpes."

"There ain't a raincoat I'd trust to go near—"

"Enough!" I snapped as I stormed back into the room. "What the fuck is the matter with you guys?"

They stared at me, eyes wide. Barkley's jaw dropped.

"All of you," I snarled. "Shut the fuck up about MA3."

No one spoke. No one moved. They didn't even blink.

"Here's a thought: why don't you all show a little respect for a fellow Sailor and a fellow MA. She's one of our own, and all you guys are doing is—" My voice cracked, and even clearing my throat wasn't enough to rein in my composure. "I'm telling you all right now, if I hear *any* of you talking like this about anyone in this command, I will make sure your ass goes to Captain's Mast. Understood?"

Nobody spoke.

"*Understood?*"

"Yes, MA2," they all murmured.

I turned around to leave and—

Stopped dead.

Stanton's eyebrows rose.

I gulped. "Sir."

"MA2." He stepped back and gestured toward his office. "Why don't we go have a little talk?"

My blood turned cold. "I . . ."

He inclined his head, the unspoken *Is that a* problem, *MA2?* sending my heart into my throat.

What else could I do? Tell him to go fuck himself? With four junior Sailors watching after I'd just handed their asses to them?

"Yes, Sir," I muttered, and obeyed.

He followed me down the hall. Good God, that was a creepy feeling. He'd always made me uncomfortable, but now that I knew what he was capable of, I could feel him leering at me from head to toe. I'd never been so thankful for the unflattering uniform and my police belt. The less he could see, the better.

I stepped into his office, and when he closed the door, my stomach lurched upward. I forced it back, though, and forced myself to keep a neutral expression as I turned to face him.

He stood in front of the door—my only escape—and folded his arms. "You seem quite protective of MA3 Lockhoff."

I took a breath. "She's a junior Sailor, Sir."

He laughed dryly. "Is that the only reason?"

"Do I need another reason?" I swallowed. "Sir?"

"Not necessarily. I'm sure she's already told you the tall tale she's spinning about what happened at Senior Chief O'Leary's retirement—"

"You're not bringing me to your side in this."

"So you do know about it?"

My blood froze.

The corner of his mouth twitched as if he was struggling not to grin. "You're a mandated reporter, MA2. You're obligated to report a sexual assault if it's reported to you." He folded his arms. "Tell me, why didn't you report it?"

I forced my voice to stay level, not daring to allow even the slightest tremor to let him know—*think*—he intimidated me. "Are you asking me to file a formal report stating that you sexually assaulted MA3 Lockhoff, Sir?"

"No, I'm not. I'm simply reminding you that you've known about this alleged 'assault,' and you've done nothing about it." He stepped closer. "So unless you'd like to go to Captain's Mast for dereliction of duty, I'd suggest you encourage your 'friend' to back down."

I drew away.

His eyes narrowed. "And I'd be happy to add a fraternization charge to that if you'd like." He raised his chin a little, glaring down at me. "Doesn't look like you're in a very good position, are you, MA2?" Before I could respond, he continued, "Especially when I'm hearing that MA3 Lockhoff has been staying with you rather than in the barracks, even though E4s aren't allowed to live off-base. Do you know anything about that?"

"I—"

"Yes or no, MA2. Is it or is it not the case that MA3 Lockhoff has been staying at your apartment?"

Though my knees were starting to shake, I held his gaze and didn't let my voice waver. "With all due respect, I'm not sure how that's anyone else's business, Sir."

"It's none of my business when one of my E4s takes it upon herself to live off-base in spite of a standing order?" He raised an eyebrow. "And a senior Sailor takes it upon herself to take her in, in violation of that order? *That's* none of my business?"

I shifted my weight. "MA3 Lockhoff doesn't feel safe on White Beach. Not here, and not in the barracks." I coughed. "Sir."

"And why doesn't she feel safe, MA2?"

I held his gaze but didn't speak.

He gestured over his shoulder. "Does it have something to do with what the other MAs are saying?" There was a note of concern in his tone, but I didn't buy it for a second. He was trying to back me into a corner, I knew it, I just didn't know where that corner was.

"What would you suggest I do, Sir? A fellow MA and junior Sailor doesn't feel safe. So I—"

"So you don't bother reporting it?"

"I—"

"And you honestly expect me to believe she's just staying there because she feels 'unsafe'?" He emphasized it with air quotes and a smirk. "You'd swear, under oath, in front of a judge and jury, that that's the *only* reason she's moved in with you since you two returned from your lengthy trip to Hawaii?"

My knees started shaking. Badly. I knew the Uniform Code of Military Justice inside and out, but under pressure, I second-guessed myself. Was he bluffing? Could he or a JAG attorney force me to admit under oath that Kim and I had a relationship?

I cleared my throat. "I told you. She's staying with me because she doesn't feel safe. That's all I—"

"Doesn't matter." Eyes narrow, he growled, "If you value your career, I would suggest you put some professional distance between the two of you."

I swallowed.

He took another step, and he was almost touching me. If I took a deep enough breath, we would touch. "Do you understand, MA2?"

My hip hit his desk.

Panic.Sheer terror. One shudder and I was back in Afghanistan. Inside a sweltering shipping container, an arm across my throat and a hand over my mouth, people talking and laughing outside with no clue what Hayes and Cunningham were doing to me.

"I asked you a question," Stanton snapped, jerking me back into the present.

I shook my head, dragging myself out of that desert shithole and back into this air-conditioned circle of hell.

And the Devil himself was still staring down at me.

I gulped. "Yes. I understand, Sir."

"Good. Now why don't you set her straight before she causes any more damage?"

All I could do was nod.

He grabbed my arm. "This conversation stays in this room. Am I clear, MA2?"

I hated myself for it, hated the way I was shaking and terrified and couldn't tell him to go fuck himself, but I just nodded silently.

He released my arm. "Dismissed, MA2."

I would've loved to convince myself that I walked out calmly, that he never saw a hint of fear. I wanted to believe he hadn't scared me, but my trembling knees and pounding heart refused to let me cling to that lie. Not even for a second.

Shit. Shit, shit, shit.

Even if he didn't have a leg to stand on, the fact was, Stanton had connections. A long reach. In the eyes of people who mattered, Kim and I were nobodies.

Someone brushed past me, and I would've kept going but Alejandro's voice stopped me in my tracks.

"MA2."

I turned around.

His forehead was creased with concern. "You all right?"

I avoided his eyes. A few weeks ago, I'd have told him everything. Now? I wasn't sure how much faith I had left in our friendship. I wanted to believe he was on our side, but as things stood, I couldn't make myself trust him any farther than I could throw him.

He reached for my arm, but I sidestepped him. "I'm fine."

"Reese, what's—"

"Oh, are we back to first names, MA1?"

He set his jaw. "Come on. Talk to me."

"I'd really rather not."

I didn't wait for a response. I walked away, and he didn't try to stop me.

I was halfway through my third cigarette when Kim pulled up. I was still jittery, my skin still crawling, but I'd calmed down a little. Hopefully enough that she wouldn't notice.

I crushed my cigarette and stepped out of the smoke pit. "Hey."

"Hey." She smiled, but it was forced. "Thanks for coming. I hope I didn't keep you waiting long."

"Don't worry about it. What's up?"

She nodded toward the building. "Let's go someplace private."

I wasn't thrilled about going back in *there*, but she didn't need to know that, so we went inside, snagged one of the classrooms beside dispatch, and closed the door.

Forcing my rattled nerves to stay beneath the surface, I hugged myself and held her gaze. "What's up?"

She mirrored me, folding her arms tight across her blue camouflage blouse. "I, um . . ."

"Whatever it is, you can tell me."

She took a deep breath. "I can't do this anymore. I *need* to report it." She rubbed the bridge of her nose and sighed. "If they charge me with a false official statement, then so be it. I'd rather make a false official statement than no statement at all."

My gut wound itself into knots and dread prickled at the base of my spine. "What about the baby? The custody threats?"

Kim shook her head. "I don't know. I don't . . ." She waved a hand. "I'm just exhausted. I can't keep carrying this secret myself, and it needs to be on paper in case he does it to someone else. If . . . if that means he might have me by the throat for the next eighteen years, then . . ."

My stomach twisted again. Stanton's voice still rang in my ears, the fear still crackling along the length of my spine. *Could* he nail us for fraternization? Misconduct?

"Reese?" She reached for my arm. "Are you onboard, or—"

"It's not my decision." I shifted uncomfortably. "If you're ready to—"

"Not by myself. I need you, Reese." She searched my eyes, hers wide with palpable desperation. "What's wrong? You were encouraging me to report it, and now . . ." Her eyebrows knitted together.

I caressed her face, thankful she couldn't hear the threats echoing through my mind just then.

And goddamn it. Goddamn *him*. He'd hurt her, and now he was threatening us both into silence?

Fuck him. Straight to hell.

I cleared my throat. "You know what? Let's go get that motherfucker."

A weak smile formed on her lips. "So you're in?"

"Damn right." I paused, and my momentary courage waned a little. "Except . . . who do you want to talk to?"

Kim's shoulders sank, and her eyes started to well up. "I don't even know. That's the problem." She waved a hand at the door. "I don't trust anyone here except you. The SARC is Stanton's golfing buddy. I . . . I don't know." She met my gaze again. "I don't know."

I gnawed my thumbnail for a moment. Then I dropped my hand and sighed. "I think your best shot is MA1 Gutiérrez."

"I thought you didn't trust him. You said he's buddy-buddy with Stanton."

I nodded. "He is. And I don't particularly trust him right now, but I trust him more than I do anyone else in our chain of command. And if . . ."

Kim inclined her head. "What?"

I sighed. "He knows the UCMJ inside and out. If he doesn't think you've got enough to pursue something against Stanton, or that this will blow up in your face, he'll tell us. And then maybe it can stop at his level instead of coming back to bite you in the ass."

"I don't *want* it to stop at his level."

"Neither do I. But if it's not going to hurt Stanton, there's no point in pursuing it to the point that it hurts you."

Kim exhaled, swearing softly.

"I'm sorry, Kim," I whispered. "I am so, so sorry."

She wiped her eyes and took a deep breath. "What do I do if Gutiérrez doesn't believe me?"

I held her gaze. I wanted to tell her there were more options. That she had more allies. More channels. But she knew as well as I did that Alejandro was her best shot. Quite possibly her only shot, with no telling if he'd even take her seriously.

I shook my head. "That's all I've got."

"Ditto." She pushed her shoulders back and cleared her throat. "I'll cross that bridge when I get there, I guess."

"Good idea." I moved closer and wrapped my arms around her.

She hugged me and whispered, "You believe me, don't you?"

"Yes." I held her tighter, squeezing my eyes shut. "And whatever happens, I'll be there. I promise."

She drew back, and our eyes met. "Thank you."

I cupped her face in my hands and pressed my lips to hers. God knew how the chips would fall, how far Stanton's reach could really extend to make both our lives hell. But he'd already made them hell, and if I lost a stripe or my career for doing everything I could to keep Kim safe and sane—or for getting involved with her like this—then so be it. It was a long shot, but we had to try to bring this asshole down.

After a moment, we separated.

I reached for the door handle. "You ready?"

She shook her head. "No. But let's do this. Let's go get him."

We held each other's gazes for a moment. Then she nodded.

And I opened the door.

CHAPTER 23
KIM

Going into an LPO's office had never been particularly scary for me. MA1 Gutiérrez was a pretty chill guy most of the time, and anyway, I didn't get in trouble so I was rarely getting chewed out.

This time, I was scared shitless. I knew the rules and regulations, and I knew I was in the right. But I also knew how much power and influence someone like Stanton had, and how little I had.

The fact that Reese didn't trust Gutiérrez anymore—especially after they'd been tight for so many years—didn't help. And if he couldn't or wouldn't help us . . .

Well, I'd cross that bridge when I got there.

We stepped into Gutiérrez's office. He'd been going over paperwork—when wasn't he, the poor bastard—and he looked up as we came in. When his gaze shifted to Reese, his jaw tightened and his eyes narrowed. "MA2. MA3. What can I do for you?"

"We need to talk to you." Reese gestured at me. "Or, well, she does."

Nothing registered on his face. "All right. Close the door and have a seat."

Reese closed the door with a quiet *click*, and we sat down in front of our boss's desk. She turned to me and nodded.

I pulled in a deep breath. This was it.

"I want to make a statement." I glanced at Reese, and when she nodded again, I faced Gutiérrez. "Against Lieutenant Stanton."

Gutiérrez's eyes widened. "For what?"

I swallowed. "Sexual assault."

As soon as the words were out, I knew this was a mistake.

"I see." One eyebrow rose, arching to ask if I was fucking serious, and then his eyes darted toward Reese. "In that case, I should get you in touch with the Sexual Assault Response—"

"I don't trust him."

He blinked. "Why not?"

"Because he plays golf with the man who raped me," I growled.

"Oh. Uh." He sat back in his chair, elbow on the armrest and a loose fist beneath his chin. "All right. When exactly did this happen?"

I moistened my lips. "Senior Chief O'Leary's retirement party." Cheeks burning, I wrung my hands in my lap. "I wasn't going to report it. I was hoping it would just go away, but then I found out I was pregnant. And I couldn't ignore it anymore."

He regarded me for a painfully long moment, eyes occasionally darting toward Reese.

Then he took a deep breath and sat up, folding his arms behind his keyboard. "I need you to tell me everything that happened, MA3. From the beginning."

I hesitated. "Do you want to write it down?"

He shook his head. "No. I want to find out what happened first. We'll proceed from there with statements."

I bristled. Beside me, Reese fidgeted but didn't speak. Facing Gutiérrez, I said, "So I have to tell you, and then if you believe me, tell you all over again?"

He chewed his lip for a moment. Finally, he reached into his desk and pulled out the familiar forms. "All right. Write everything down. Everything you remember. Date, time, witnesses, everything."

I resisted the urge to snark back that I was well aware how statements were handled. It didn't matter if he'd deliberately insulted my intelligence or not—at least he wasn't stopping me from giving the statement.

Neither of them spoke while I wrote everything down. By the time I'd finished, I was sweating bullets, and when I handed the form back, my hand was shaking a little.

Then there was more silence as Gutiérrez read my statement and I tried to read him. Was he just concentrating? Or did those creases in his forehead mean he was ready to raise the bullshit flag?

Eventually, he set the report down. "Why haven't you reported it until now? I get that you waited until you found out you were pregnant, but even that was quite a while ago."

I shifted in my chair. "Because I was scared."

"Of . . .?" He leaned forward, folding his hands on the desk. "Retaliation?"

"Yeah. I mean, like I said, he plays golf with the SARC. And the Captain."

"How do you know that?"

"Because Stanton *told* me."

"He told . . ." Gutiérrez's eyes flicked back and forth between us. "Did he know you were planning to make the accusation?"

I nodded. "He made sure to threaten me with everything from his connections to the baby to my lack of credibility."

"Lack of credibility? How so?"

"He insists I have none because of my reputation for sleeping around."

He held my gaze, a mix of confusion and disbelief in his eyes.

"She's not a slut," Reese said, breaking her long silence. "Even if she was, that doesn't excuse anything, but if Stanton wants to use her sexual behavior to *try* to excuse it, then the burden of proof is on him. And the fact is, he has no proof."

"Neither do you," Gutiérrez said quietly to me.

I sat up. "Find me one single man on this island who'll swear under oath he's ever had sex with me, and I'll drop this. In fact, any man. Anywhere.Navy or not. Find *one*, and I'll never bring it up again."

He eyed me. Though he didn't say it, the skepticism was etched into the creases on his forehead.

"It doesn't make a difference," Reese growled. "Even if she *were* as promiscuous as everyone says she is, that doesn't give him the right to—"

"I'm aware of the law." Gutiérrez looked at me. "Where are you going with this?"

I forced myself to hold his gaze. "You'll never find any man who'll swear under oath they've slept with me because I'm a lesbian."

He blinked. "You are?"

"Yes. I've never even had sex with a man. Except . . ." I shuddered.

"I see. And you said he tried to threaten you with the baby?"

I nodded. "He coerced me into getting an abortion. Or, well, he tried to."

Gutiérrez watched me for a moment. "That's why you went to Hawaii, isn't it?"

"Yeah."

His gaze shifted to Reese. "And you went there to . . .?"

"She needed support." Reese took my hand, and MA1 didn't seem at all surprised by that. "Which I gave her. And ultimately, she decided against the abortion."

"I see." He glanced at our hands, then me. "Unofficially, it was my understanding that you and Stanton had agreed that abortion was the best option." He ran his thumbnail along his lower lip. "What changed your mind?"

"It was never my decision in the first place. Stanton . . . he told me there was no other choice." I exhaled hard, my heart pounding. "He said if I didn't get the abortion, he wouldn't consent to giving the baby up for adoption unless I didn't press charges. And if I do press charges, and he forces me to keep it, he's going to demand visitation. No jury will ever convict him, so when he gets off, he'll make my life a living hell."

Gutiérrez's eyes were huge. He sank back against his chair. "This is a tough spot, MA3. We can prove you and Stanton had sex—"

I clenched my teeth, barely keeping myself from vomiting.

His eyebrows rose a little. "We can prove that much, but we can't prove that there was no consent."

"So it's just his word against mine. I don't have any injuries or scars, and no one saw me trying to stop him, so . . . that's it."

He sighed. "You're a cop, MA3. You know what position I'm in here."

"With all due respect, what I don't know is if you're in that position because it's a hard case to prove or because you're taking his word over mine."

His posture stiffened. "Look, I'm in this to protect my Sailors. If someone's done any of you wrong, I wouldn't be doing my job if I wasn't objective about the situation."

"*Are* you being objective about it?" Reese asked.

Their eyes met, and the temperature in the room plummeted.

"Listen," I broke in before they could start arguing, "I'm not doing this for fun, okay? I don't want to risk my career or fuck myself over. All I want is to be a cop and to be in the Navy. That's all I've ever wanted. I'm not going to jeopardize that just to have a fling with an officer, and I'm not going to throw it away over a false statement." I sat up straighter and held MA1's gaze. "I'm doing this because if I don't press charges against him, then sooner or later, he's going to do it again. This won't change what happened to me, but maybe I'll be able to sleep at night if I know he won't do it to someone else. And judging by what his wife said to me today, I think he's done it before."

"Wait, what?" Gutiérrez leaned forward. "His wife?"

I nodded. "She came into Pass & ID to warn me against filing charges. She said he's cheated before, but he's not a rapist. And it occurred to me that if he's cheated before, there's a good chance O'Leary's retirement wasn't his first time doing it without consent."

Reese squeezed my hand, and we exchanged glances.

Gutiérrez turned to Reese. "Now, you say you've known about this?"

She hesitated but nodded.

"For how long?"

"Since . . ." She set her shoulders back, as if steeling herself. "Since the day you asked me to take her to medical."

His eyebrows rose. "And you didn't say anything? Even though you're—"

"A mandated reporter. I know." She took a breath. "I'll accept full responsibility for that part. If you want to hem me up for dereliction of duty, fine. I only did it because I knew she needed someone, and she didn't have anyone else on this island." Reese swallowed hard, eyes locked on Gutiérrez. "And there was a time when I would have killed for someone who'd listen to me and believe me."

Gutiérrez's lips parted and his eyes widened. "You . . ."

"I've been there," Reese whispered. "And after she's looked me in the eye and told me what Stanton did to her, I believe her beyond a shadow of a doubt."

Gutiérrez exhaled slowly. His eyes darted back and forth between us.

"And Stanton hasn't just threatened Lockhoff."

"*What?*" Gutiérrez and I both said.

Reese fidgeted, looking down at her wringing hands. "He pulled me into his office earlier." She glanced at me. "A little while before you got here. And he . . . Basically, he said that if she filed a report, he'd make sure I was strung up for fraternization and allowing an E4 to live off-base. And he kind of . . ." She sighed and rubbed her eyes. "He caught me off guard and got me to admit I knew about the allegation." She looked across the desk at Gutiérrez. "And if Kim reported it, then he was going to charge me with dereliction of duty and failure to report an assault."

"Are you serious?" Gutiérrez breathed.

Barely whispering, she said, "Yes."

Gutiérrez sat back. His gaze moved from the statement, to our joined hands, to Reese, to me, to the statement. The silence went on and on and on. I couldn't breathe. It felt like my entire world was hanging in the balance, my future tucked into the crevices between his eyebrows.

All at once, he slammed his fist down on the desk so hard, Reese and I both jumped and the keyboard bounced. "That son of a *bitch*." Facing me, he leaned forward. "MA3, look me in the eye and tell me everything you've stated and everything in this"—he tapped my statement—"is true."

I looked right at him. "Everything is true. Lieutenant Stanton raped me, and he's the father of my baby." I swallowed the nausea trying to rise in my throat. "And he tried to coerce me into an abortion and threatened me if I reported him."

Gutiérrez chewed his thumbnail for a moment, then met my eyes. "If you ladies will give me a second, I need to make a phone call."

My throat tightened. I glanced at Reese, and when she nodded, I said, "Uh, okay."

Gutiérrez picked up the phone. "This is MA1 Gutiérrez. May I speak with Captain Falk, please? I'll hold."

My heart was going crazy now. I felt around until my fingers met Reese's. She grabbed on, her palm sweaty, and squeezed gently.

Gutiérrez glanced at our hands again. Then his eyes lost focus. "Sir, this is MA1 Gutiérrez. I'm calling to inform you that I'm placing Lieutenant Stanton under arrest."

My jaw fell open. Reese gripped my hand tighter, and we exchanged stunned glances.

A second later, Gutiérrez set the phone down. "All right. Let's do this." He rose, withdrawing a set of handcuffs from his police belt. He glanced at them, then at me. "Since you're a cop, I'd let you do this, but you're also the victim so I can't."

"I know." Why was I shaking so badly?

Gutiérrez turned to Reese. "You want to do the honors?"

She hesitated. "But he threatened me—"

"That'll come out during questioning." He dangled the cuffs off his thumb and grinned. "Doesn't mean I knew about it when I sent you in to arrest the fucker for assaulting her."

Reese glanced at me. Then she returned his grin and held out her hand. "I would *love* to."

CHAPTER 24
REESE

had never been so thrilled to be at Lieutenant Stanton's door.

I knocked sharply.

"Now's not a good time," came the terse response.

"Sir, I need you to open the door."

Other voices murmured inside the office. Familiar ones, though quiet enough I couldn't immediately place them.

"Sir, please open the door or I'll open it."

The men on the other side laughed.

"I'm in a meeting, MA2." He sounded so damned condescending, I could almost feel him rolling his eyes and gesturing at the door as if to say, *Can you believe this?*

Beside me, Alejandro grumbled something. Kim shifted her weight—I could only imagine how this situation made her feel.

And I wasn't interested in dragging it out any longer.

I turned the knob and stepped into the room. Senior Chief Brighton and Chief Wolcott were sitting in front of his desk, but I didn't hesitate. "Lieutenant Stanton, I need you to stand up, turn around, and put your hands behind your head."

"I beg your pardon?" Stanton laughed, and he didn't move.

"What in the world is this about?" Senior Chief asked. "This is—"

"Lieutenant Stanton." I held up the cuffs. "Turn around. Put your hands behind your head."

He looked past me. "MA1, what the hell are—" His eyes narrowed. "*You're* behind all of this, aren't you, MA3?"

"I'm not going to ask again," I said coolly. "Turn around—"

He snorted. "I don't take orders from second-class petty officers."

A sharp metallic *thunk* turned my head, and I glanced back to see that Alejandro had taken out and extended his baton. He held it by his leg, opening and closing his fingers menacingly. "She's not going to ask you again, Sir, and neither am I."

Stanton was about to speak, but Senior Chief beat him to it. "Uh, Sir, why don't you cooperate, and we'll see if this can't be sorted out peacefully?" He shot Alejandro a *Won't we?* look.

I took a step toward Stanton. He glared at me but then cursed under his breath and turned around.

"Hands behind your head, Sir."

"MA2, we've talked about—"

"Hands behind your head *now*, Sir."

He pushed out a huff of breath but wisely laced his fingers behind his head. I grabbed his arm, brought it down to the small of his back, and closed the first cuff around his wrist.

And Stanton lost his shit.

He jerked away from me and spun around. His fist came out of nowhere, connecting with my face and sending me back a step.

Everyone else in the room lunged forward—whether to restrain me or him, I couldn't be sure—but I was faster. I shoved Stanton back against the wall hard enough to make him grunt. While he was still off-balance, I spun him around, slammed him chest first into the wall, and twisted his arm behind him.

"You done?" I growled in his ear.

"Fuck you," he snarled, just loud enough for me and no one else.

I twisted his arm harder, driving another grunt out of him. "That's not exactly conduct becoming an officer and a gentleman, is it?"

He swore and struggled between my body and the wall, but I just cranked his arm harder.

"You really want to add resisting arrest to your—"

His heel connected with my shin, and in the split second that I was startled, he tried to jerk his arm free, but I gripped it tighter, twisted it harder, and shoved him against the wall again. Before he could recover from that, I jerked him back toward me and kicked his knee out from under him. He went down. I went with him. His kneecap cracked loudly on the hard floor, and he cried out in pain as I shoved him forward onto his face.

I put my knee between his shoulder blades and leaned over him. "Are we done here, *Sir?*"

He didn't speak, but he also didn't struggle. He touched his forehead to the floor, and I could feel the fight leaving him. He'd been a cop during his enlisted days—he knew as well as I did that he'd lose if he tried anything now.

I jerked his other arm back and cuffed it. As I helped him to his feet, I recited his Miranda rights. "You're under arrest for Article 120, sexual assault. Article—"

"Sexual assault?" He glared at Kim. "Oh, spare me. You'd have given it up sooner or later, you fucking whore."

Everyone in the room froze. Chief and Senior Chief glanced at each other.

"Come on, asshole." Alejandro grabbed Stanton's arm. To me, he said, "You two meet me in my office." Then he started toward the door with Stanton. "Lieutenant Joel Stanton, you are under arrest for violations of Article 133 of the Military Rules of Evidence, unlawful command influence and coercion. Article 120 of the UCMJ, sexual assault. Article 120 again, assault on a police officer. Article 134, adultery . . ."

As they disappeared down the hall, through the gauntlet of wide-eyed MAs who'd gathered, Alejandro was *still* reading off charges.

Kim released a breath and sagged against the wall, closing her eyes and letting her head fall back. I stepped closer and touched her shoulder. "You okay?"

"Yeah." She blinked a few times and looked up at me. "What about you? How's your—" She gestured at her mouth.

I dabbed at mine and came away with a bit of blood but nothing alarming. "I'll be all right." I nodded in the direction he'd gone. "I don't think he'll feel so great in the morning."

"Sucks to be him." She rubbed her forehead. "I can't decide if I'm relieved or scared shitless of what's going to happen next."

"Whatever happens, you know you've got my support. And MA1's."

"I know." She smiled up at me. "Thank you."

I returned the smile and hugged her gently.

Behind us, Senior Chief cleared his throat. "MA3 Lockhoff, why don't you take MA2 Marion over to medical and have that looked at?" He shifted uncomfortably. "While you're there, I'll send someone up to get statements from both of you. I'd . . . like to make sure this is all properly documented."

We both nodded and murmured, "Yes, Senior Chief."

Reese hesitated. "Could you let MA1 Gutiérrez know we'll come to his office when we get back? He wanted us to wait for him."

Senior Chief nodded. "I'll do that."

"Thank you, Senior Chief."

By the time Kim and I came back from medical, every MA on Okinawa must have known. There were usually a few of the guys hanging around the precinct, but there were at least fifteen this time.

As we walked in, they made room, and I kept my focus straight ahead. None of them said a word.

A few feet from Alejandro's door, Kim paused. "Damn it, pregnant girl's gotta pee. I'll be right back."

I laughed. "Go ahead. I'll meet you in here."

She went one way, and I went the other. Alejandro was waiting in his office, and as soon as I walked in, he said, "How's your lip?"

I played at it with my tongue. "It'll heal. Looks a lot worse than it is."

"That's good. Looked like he hit you pretty hard."

I shrugged. "His mistake."

Alejandro chuckled.

"I'm guessing he wasn't happy about being booked?"

"Jesus, no." Alejandro whistled. "I've seen drunk Marines who were less belligerent."

"If I'd had another minute or so with him, I probably could've made him cry like that drunk lance corporal we brought in last month."

Alejandro laughed. "Well, when we told him his wife had been contacted and the CO was on his way down, he turned white. I'll bet he'll cry once they get here."

"Pity I won't get to see that."

"Eh, you probably wouldn't want to."

"Probably not."

He studied me for a moment. "I, uh, after everything you and Lockhoff told me today, I can see why you were so upset with me last time we talked."

"I wasn't being fair. You didn't know."

"I didn't, but . . ." He sighed. "I could've done more for her."

"You got her out of this office." I managed a smile, albeit a lopsided one since the side of my mouth hurt like hell. "And when it came down to it, you believed her. That's the important part."

"I still feel like an ass. But . . . thanks. For trusting me even after you thought you couldn't."

"We had to. You were the only person we had left."

He swallowed hard. "I hope that's not the only reason."

"No. No, I guess it wasn't."

"And, uh, if I had known . . ."

"I know. I would've told you, but . . ." I shook my head. "She didn't want to report it yet and I—"

"I don't just mean about her. Why didn't you ever tell me what happened to you?"

I avoided his eyes. "I never told anyone. Aside from Kim, I mean."

He pulled me into a tight embrace. "I am so sorry."

"It's not your fault." I exhaled and hugged him, relieved that I had my friend back. "You know it's not."

"Still." He released me and looked me in the eye. "You can trust me. As your friend and your LPO."

"Thank you," I whispered.

Kim appeared in the doorway. She glanced back and forth between us. "Am I, uh, interrupting?"

"Not at all." Alejandro gestured for her to come in. As she closed the door behind her, he said, "Do you two need to add anything? To your statements?"

We both shook our heads.

Kim shifted her weight. "I don't have anything to add, but . . . what happens next?" She waved a hand. "I mean, I know how investigations work. But I'm kind of afraid he's going to . . ."

"Use his influence and connections to weasel out of this?" Alejandro asked.

"Yeah. Exactly."

"Well, between resisting arrest, assaulting MA2 Marion, and that little comment he made on the way out the door, all with multiple witnesses?" Alejandro shook his head. "That motherfucker is *done*."

"Thank God," Kim breathed and leaned against the wall. "Fuck." She wiped at her eyes, and I embraced her.

"Hey. You okay?"

She nodded and sniffed as she hugged me back. "Just . . . can't believe it's over."

I stroked her hair. Of course, it wasn't completely over—the investigation and trial would be hell—but she'd finally dropped the hammer and reported Stanton. He wasn't merrily going about his life while she lost sleep over the secret she'd been coerced into keeping. It was a huge weight off my shoulders; I could only imagine how much had been lifted off hers.

Alejandro cleared his throat. "There's just a bit more paperwork before you go. Since Reese is the arresting officer . . . Well, you know the drill. Once that's all squared away, why don't the two of you take the rest of the day off?"

Kim smirked. "I'm technically *already* off."

"Well pin a rose on your nose." I elbowed her playfully. "Some of us are still on shift for a couple of hours."

Alejandro laughed. "You know what? Just come in first thing in the morning, and we'll wrap everything up. I'll get Navy Legal and JAG on the horn and make sure you've got all the support you need for the investigation."

Kim drew back from me and smiled at him. "Thank you, MA1."

He put up his hands. "Hey, don't thank me. You two are the ones who had the brass balls to take Stanton down, even after he threatened you. All I did was call the CO."

"Still," I said. "Thank you."

He nodded. "Don't mention it. And if *anyone* gives either of you shit about this investigation, come straight to me. Understood?"

"Understood," we said in unison.

He dismissed us, and we didn't wait around. We left his office and walked out of the freezing-cold precinct into the heavy tropical heat.

Kim put her cover back on and took a long, deep breath through her nose. "God, I am so glad that part's over."

"Me too. Let's get the fuck out of here."

"You want to grab a cigarette before we go?"

I glanced at the smoke pit, and . . . nothing. Not even the slightest pull.

"No. I smoke when I'm stressed." I smiled at her. "But right now, I feel pretty damned good."

"Funny how that works." She slipped her hand into mine. "What do you say we go change out of our uniforms, find a beach somewhere, and just chill for the afternoon?"

"That's a fucking awesome idea." I squeezed her hand and, with my other, pulled my car keys from my pocket. "Let's go."

EPILOGUE
KIM

Several Months Later

Standing in front of the bathroom mirror, I ran my hand over the front of my camouflage blouse. It felt strange to be in uniform again. Even stranger than not having that huge belly anymore.

I barely recognized myself. I'd gotten so used to being heavily made-up whenever I was in uniform, wearing a blouse just tight enough to show off my tits, it was weird to look in the bathroom mirror and see . . . this. Still a little round in the cheeks from the baby weight, but otherwise, the woman looking back at me was the one my old command had dubbed Razor Wire. Just enough makeup to cover up the dark circles under my eyes—at least I'd been sleeping better lately—with a touch of mascara and some lip liner.

It felt good to be back in my own skin. The way I'd presented myself before hadn't been an invitation for Stanton, but it had also never been . . . me. The way I looked now wasn't necessarily me, either. Maybe it was, maybe it wasn't. Maybe now I could finally figure that out.

I'd had the baby a month and a half ago, and the first couple of weeks had been rough. Knowing I was doing the right thing hadn't made giving him up any easier, but I was getting better. Day by day, a little at a time, I was getting better.

The baby was in good hands now. I'd recovered physically. The trial was over.

That trial had been a shitstorm if there'd ever been one. Stanton's attorney had tried to use my reputation against me, and he'd tried to nail Reese for dereliction of duty, failure to report, and fraternization, but the JAG prosecutor wasn't having it. Under the circumstances, Reese's failure to report had been deemed reasonable and justified, and even the fraternization charges couldn't stick since Reese wasn't technically my supervisor.

The prosecutor had eviscerated the defense up one side and down the other, and the guilty verdict hadn't surprised anyone. Especially not after the prosecutor had presented some surprising—and extremely damning—character witnesses. Word about Stanton's arrest had traveled fast, and within two weeks, three other women—including one who was now a respected senior chief at another command— had come forward. Though they'd only heard that he'd been accused of sexual assault, their stories were eerily similar to mine. A party. A few drinks. Just enough force to make it clear there was no point in resisting unless she wanted to get hurt.

I'd had a feeling there were others, but it still blew my mind when they came forward and confirmed it. I wasn't alone. I hadn't imagined it. The pattern was clearly established, and his guilt was undeniable.

Stanton had been shipped off to Leavenworth, where he'd lose his rank and be reduced to "Prisoner" and a number, and where he'd never bother any of us again. Before he'd transferred to the prison, where he'd remain until he was an old, old man, he'd been ordered to terminate his parental rights. By the time I'd had the baby, Stanton was gone, and I was free and clear of him. The baby was now making a young lieutenant commander and his wife very happy after they'd struggled for six long years to have one of their own.

Reese stepped into the bathroom, drawing me out of my thoughts, and grinned. "Looking good, sweetie."

I met her eyes in the mirror and smiled. "Feels good to put it on again."

"I'll bet it does." She wrapped her arms around me from behind. "You ready for this?"

I took a deep breath. "I think so."

"Nervous?"

"A little. I'm still not sure what the other MAs are going to think."

"Well, I doubt they'll fuck with you." She kissed my cheek. "If anything, they're probably *scared* to fuck with you. The whole command is still impressed as hell that you took Stanton down."

I smiled and leaned against her. "God. I am so glad he's gone."

"Me too. The command climate has changed a lot, too."

"So you've said."

"Still plenty of bullshit, though, so let's get moving." She kissed my cheek once more, then released me. "I need coffee before I face any of these assholes."

I smirked. "Maybe we should quit staying up so late, then."

"No, I didn't say that." She winked. "I just need some coffee to deal with the aftermath."

"Fair enough."

"Good. Let's go."

"All right, I'll be there in a second."

She left the bathroom, and I glanced in the mirror one more time. No, I definitely didn't look anything like the girl I'd been a year ago. The guys I'd worked with probably wouldn't know what to make of this one.

Well, I guess they'd figure it out.

I turned off the light and headed out with Reese.

My maternity leave was over. My rapist was guilty and gone.

I was a cop again. My son was in good hands. My girlfriend was still by my side.

And my life was finally mine again.

Dear Reader,

Thank you for reading Lauren Gallagher's *Razor Wire*!

We know your time is precious and you have many, many entertainment options, so it means a lot that you've chosen to spend your time reading. We really hope you enjoyed it.

We'd be honored if you'd consider posting a review—good or bad—on sites like **Amazon, Barnes & Noble, Kobo, Goodreads, Twitter, Facebook, Tumblr,** and your blog or website. We'd also be honored if you told your friends and family about this book. Word of mouth is a book's lifeblood!

For more information on upcoming releases, author interviews, blog tours, contests, giveaways, and more, please sign up for our weekly, spam-free newsletter and visit us around the web:

Newsletter: tinyurl.com/RiptideSignup
Twitter: twitter.com/RiptideBooks
Facebook: facebook.com/RiptidePublishing
Goodreads: tinyurl.com/RiptideOnGoodreads
Tumblr: riptidepublishing.tumblr.com

Thank you so much for Reading the Rainbow!

RiptidePublishing.com

ACKNOWLEDGMENTS

This book wouldn't have been possible without several MAs and other military personnel who thoroughly answered my seemingly never-ending list of questions and patiently walked me through the hypothetical scenarios that eventually became this story. You all know who you are. Thank you.

ALSO BY
LAUREN GALLAGHER

ABOUT THE AUTHOR

Lauren Gallagher is an abnormal romance writer currently living in the wilds of Omaha, Nebraska. She and her husband, along with a coyote-iguana hybrid and two and a half cats, are thought to be in hiding from the Polynesian Mafia and a debt collector in search of a fine for an overdue book from the Library of Alexandria. Lauren continues to skillfully, if somewhat clumsily, elude them, but continues to have run-ins with her archnemesis, M/M erotic romance author L.A. Witt. The implementation of Operation: I Don't Think So is expected to resolve that problem soon enough.

Website: www.loriawitt.com
Twitter: @GallagherWitt
Blog: gallagherwitt.blogspot.com

Enjoy this book?
Find more lesbian fiction at
RiptidePublishing.com!

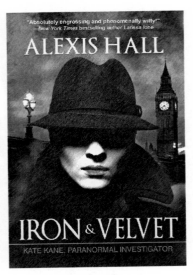

The Beginning of Us
ISBN: 978-1-62649-105-2

Iron & Velvet
ISBN: 978-1-62649-049-9

Earn Bonus Bucks!

Earn 1 Bonus Buck for each dollar you spend. Find out how at RiptidePublishing.com/news/bonus-bucks.

Win Free Ebooks for a Year!

Pre-order coming soon titles directly through our site and you'll receive one entry into a drawing to win free books for a year! Get the details at RiptidePublishing.com/contests.

CPSIA information can be obtained
at www.ICGtesting.com
Printed in the USA
FSOW01n1205110915
10998FS

9 781626 491885